Frances Elliot

The Ill-Tempered Cousin

Vol. III

Frances Elliot

The Ill-Tempered Cousin
Vol. III

ISBN/EAN: 9783337066581

Printed in Europe, USA, Canada, Australia, Japan

Cover: Foto ©Andreas Hilbeck / pixelio.de

More available books at **www.hansebooks.com**

THE ILL-TEMPERED COUSIN.

THE ILL-TEMPERED COUSIN.

A NOVEL.

BY

FRANCES ELLIOT,

AUTHOR OF 'DIARY OF AN IDLE WOMAN IN SPAIN'
'THE RED CARDINAL,' ETC.

IN THREE VOLUMES.

VOL. III.

LONDON: F. V. WHITE & CO.,
31 SOUTHAMPTON STREET, STRAND, W.C.

1885.

COLSTON AND SON, PRINTERS, EDINBURGH.

THE ILL-TEMPERED COUSIN.

CHAPTER I.

IN the general silence which ensued, the sound of John's departing footsteps echoed through the hall. Then the front door shut with a bang, and all was still.

'Tell me,' said Lady Danvers, after a pause, a somewhat softer intonation in her high-set voice, 'have you any other attachment to account for this?'

In an instant a burning blush mantled on Sophia's cheeks. She stretched out her hands imploringly.

'I had rather not say,' she faltered. 'I beg you not to ask.'

'Certainly not,' answered Lady Danvers coldly; 'but I am sorry to find you put no confidence in those who have a right to know.'

With these words, the remembrance of Edward Maitland's message flashed across Mrs Winter. It must be for his sake she had refused John Bauer. It was his absence which was driving her to despair. By her culpable silence she had unconsciously brought about this scene; but if her whole life depended on it, she could not at that moment have summoned courage to tell her.

'May I speak?' said a faltering voice, as Jane timidly stole over to where her mother was standing. 'Dear mamma, I beg your pardon for daring to interfere, but oh! the whole happiness of my life is at stake.'

'What do you mean, child?' said Lady Danvers, sharply, bringing her glass to bear on the alarmed eyes of Jane, raised to hers in an agony of entreaty.

'I mean—I mean,' she said, turning now red, now white, 'that I am alone at home, except the dog Nep, and he does not count—quite alone, mamma. I love Sophia dearly; I think I understand her.

Could she not come to us, until she has made up her mind ? You have always been so good to me when I have asked you anything in earnest. And you are Sophia's aunt, mamma, the same as Aunt Amelia.'

Never did a few short sentences cause such a commotion. Lady Danvers, who had evidently never dreamt of such a proposal, turned away with an angry frown.

Sophia, fixing her eyes first on Jane, then on Lady Danvers, was uncertain what to say. Aunt Amelia started to her feet, and Uncle Louis, by a violent jerk, presented his back to the company, with a grimace of intense disgust.

'This is a mad scheme,' said Lady Danvers, after a painful silence. 'I suppose' (to Jane) 'you and Sophia have concocted it together.'

An ominous cloud darkened her brow.

'No, no!' cried an eager, young voice, and a pair of clasped hands were thrust forward. 'I have not even told Sophia.'

'No, indeed, Lady Danvers,' from Sophia, the astonishment of whose looks backed up her words. 'I never heard of it before.'

'Well, be that as it may, it is asking of

me a most unwarrantable sacrifice. You
hardly know Sophia, Jane.'

'Oh yes, indeed I do, mamma ; I know
her, and I love her.'

('Dear, generous little cousin,' murmured
Sophia, drawing her eager face to hers
and kissing it ,' it is no use.' Jane, in
the same low tone,—'No use, Sophia!
We shall see. No one can resist you,
not even mamma.')

'A most unexpected proposal,' continued Lady Danvers, after a pause, during
which she reflected that Sophia would, in
all probability, shortly marry, and that a
temporary residence under her roof would
give her a much better chance of doing so
creditably, than the protection of such a
man as Louis Winter. Then turning to
Mrs Winter, who had never moved from
her seat,—'I would gladly relieve you,
dear Amelia, from the presence of Sophia.
I see you do not get on ; but it seems to
me she will not like a residence with me
any better. You are all gentleness ; a
great deal too yielding. In my house,
I take into consideration no peculiarities
of temper, or accidents of position. Those
who enter my door as inmates must con-
form to my rules. Because Sophia is a

motherless girl I can make no exception
for her. No, Jane. No!'—putting back
from her eager Jane, whose face was
streaming with tears — 'don't be silly.
There is no use crying in that violent
way. You have sacrificed me enough
already to your foolish fancy without
making a scene. Let Sophia decide for
herself.'

Sophia was brave; she was almost heroic, but her heart sank within her as she
contemplated the stony expression of Lady
Danvers' handsome face; but, stung by
the recollection of that insulting letter,
which had not only deprived her of Edward, but had set all her old wounds
bleeding afresh, she was conscious of but
one overwhelming longing, and that was
to escape far from the scene of her
degradation. No spot on earth could
humiliate her as much as Twickenham.

'I understand you,' she replied, in a
voice out of which all expression was
gone, 'and I accept. If you will allow
me, I will come to you on a visit. I fear
I am not sufficiently grateful. I have
been differently brought up. People in
India are not ashamed of their poor
relations. Even the animals and plants

are cared for ; they may contain a human soul.'

The implied sneer of these words went far to extinguish that nascent interest Lady Danvers had begun to feel for her ; but too wise to be drawn into any further altercation, she passed them by.

'You have spoken very plainly,' continued Sophia ; 'I will be equally so. Be kind enough to form no plans for my future life, as Mrs Winter has done. I would rather beg than accept a man I do not love.'

This was too much for Louis Winter. Although scrupulously conscious of his duties as host, this breaking up of all his brilliant schemes for Sophia's marriage, not only to be the making of *her*, but, from his nephew's well - known liberality, sure to be largely beneficial to his own pocket, he threw up his hands with a frantic gesture, and exclaimed,—

'Tausend teufels! die Sophie ees von lunatics! Die tamned Danvers have got her vay!' and in a burst of uncontrollable fury, rushed from the room.

His wife watched his exit with dismay. It was too much to hope her sister had not heard him; but, at all events, the moment had come when, now or never, she must deliver Edward Maitland's message. So, leaving Lady Danvers' side, to whom she had instinctively clung for help in this crisis, with a deprecatory action, she placed her hand on Sophia's arm.

'You are so angry with me, dear, already,' she began, suffering acutely under the battery of Sophia's black eyes, which expressed most clearly how little intercourse she desired, 'I almost fear you will never forgive me; but the fact is, I suffer so much from palpitation, I really was unable yesterday to speak.'

'To what subject do you refer?' asked Sophia, instinctively drawing back (she was longing to be alone, quiet, in her own room).

'Ah! I forgot,' said poor Aunt Amelia, reddening. 'You do not know. Well, yesterday, just as I was coming in, I met Mr Maitland outside the door, and he stopped me, and said,—" Tell Miss Escott "—'

'I do not believe one word of it!' cried Sophia, her face suddenly crimson. 'This is one of your inventions, Mrs Winter. Mr Maitland would never,—no never, have spoken of me to you!'

'But, I assure you,' insisted Mrs Winter, now filled with apprehension at the mischief her ill-advised silence had brought about,' he did indeed; and he said, "Tell Miss Escott I am going away, but—"'

'There is no question of Mr Maitland any longer,' broke in Sophia, the words of the letter rising like fire before her eyes. 'What is he to me? A stranger! What right has he to deliver messages to you? Mr Maitland, indeed! Just now it was Mr Bauer. I altogether decline to receive any messages while I remain here!' and with these imperious words, and a still more imperious glance, the haughty girl dashed hastily out of the room, running full against Jacob in the dark passage, with his ear to the keyhole.

'Lord a mussy!' cried he, bursting, with terrified looks, into the room.

'Who's that? I thought it war a ghost.' Then, finding himself full in the centre of the company, he suddenly came to his senses, and, pulling at a lock in the middle of his forehead, bowed.

'Please ma'am,' to Mrs Winter, 'there's a visitor in the drawing-room. (Now, Jacob knew it was low to pull his hair, and that it was only done by linkmen and beggars, but in moments of excitement early habits prevailed.)

'A visitor!' exclaimed Aunt Amelia aghast, hastily drying her eyes. 'Why, it is quite dark! Who can it be?'

'Can't you say you are not at home?' suggested Lady Danvers.

'No, marm,' put in Jacob; 'I tellt her the missus wur in the Dragon-room, along with the little miss. Then says she, she says, "Tell the lady I am come to call on her sister, Lady Danvers," meaning you, mum.'

'Who is it, Jacob?' asked Mrs Winter, still drawing back.

'Mrs Maitland, mum, she as lives at Rosebank; we serves her with cauliflowers, we do, when them's run short.'

'Oh!' cried Mrs Winter, helplessly
sinking on a chair. 'After this dreadful scene, do help me. I cannot face
Mrs Maitland alone. She always insults
me. Heaven knows what she will
say!'

'Nothing unbecoming while I am
present,' answered Lady Danvers, with
that calm voice which always reassured
her sister. 'Vulgar woman! Much as
I dislike her, I will go.'

It might be thought that, after that
interview with her son, Mrs Maitland
ought not to have come, but no one
would have said so who saw the meeting,
the cringing politeness with which she
received the cold greeting of Lady Danvers, and the anxious civility with which
she accosted Mrs Winter.

It is true that she did feel, under the
circumstances, that she ought to cut
the whole Scatlands' party; but her longing for facts prevailed. Miss Sterne had
become so absent and silent she could get
nothing out of her at all. Edward had
not written, and Mrs Shorne had aggra-
vated her by hinting that she supposed
Lady Danvers looked down on the
Twickenham people too much to receive

them. This decided her. 'Not receive
me!' retorted Mrs Maitland, 'after the
shameful conspiracy in which they have
all engaged to rob me of my son! It
is *I* that confer a favour on her by
going.'

'It is rather unusual, I fear, to break
into a family party on Christmas Day,'
observed Mrs Maitland, taking a com-
prehensive view round, to satisfy herself that the obnoxious Sophia was not
concealed somewhere ; 'but I was anxious
to pay my respects to you, Lady Danvers, on the earliest possible occasion.'

'It is not my habit to receive visitors
when from home,' was her reply, with
a frigid bow. 'I only allow myself to
make an exception towards my sister's
friends. You have, however, I understand,' said Lady Danvers, eyeing the
stout full-blown matron before her, positively bristling in the richest silks, with
no friendly glance, 'seen but little of my
sister lately, and my new niece not at all.
She is a beautiful creature. The last time
I met you, you were so deeply interested
about her.'

With Lady Danvers' eye upon her, Mrs

Maitland began to repent that she had come. From red she turned to scarlet, and grew hot to her finger-ends.

'It is just that,' she said hastily, giving Aunt Amelia a supplicating glance. 'I felt that, knowing all about Miss Escott as I did' (and here, social coward as she was, she plucked up a little courage, and accentuated these words), 'I could not delay offering my congratulations on her approaching marriage, so very fortunate, under the peculiar circumstances. Mrs Winter and I have often talked them over.'

'To what marriage do you allude?' asked Lady Danvers, deliberately adjusting her eyeglass and contemplating Mrs Maitland with such a frigid stare, that she intuitively felt she had delivered herself up into the hands of an adversary too strong for her.

'Why, of course the marriage of Miss Escott with Mr Bauer' (moving uneasily in her chair); 'such a godsend for poor Mrs Winter, after all the dreadful things which have happened.'

'I am not aware that anything has happened,' replied Lady Danvers, growing more and more displeased; 'Sophia has had the misfortune to lose her father. She has come to England under the protection of her family; specially of mine,' she added, putting down her glass, and turning over her sparkling diamond rings, with a movement natural to her. 'As to her marriage, you are under a mistake, Mrs Maitland; no such idea exists. My niece leaves with me for Faulds at the conclusion of my visit; she will be a pleasant companion for my daughter.'

Poor Mrs Maitland was utterly dumbfounded; she had not the tact to hide it.

Mrs Winter listened, with an irrepressible twinkle in her eye. It was astonishing what a sense of humour the little woman had, when backed up by her sister. (Heart-broken as she had been at Sophia's rejection of John Bauer, now that she had had time to reflect on the possibility of a return to her former quiet life by Sophia's departure, she was not without consolation. After all, why despair? Her sister was so clever, there was no saying what might happen.)

'I suppose Mr Edward is with you for

Christmas?' was slyly asked by Aunt Amelia, with a smile.

Now this was not to be borne. Even before Lady Danvers, Mrs Maitland could not command herself.

'No, Mrs Winter, he is not with us, and you know it,' was her answer, bridling with ill-concealed anger, 'and the cause.'

'Am I to understand that his absence has anything to do with my niece?' asked Lady Danvers (determined, as she afterwards said, to put down that pretentious, low-bred woman). 'You did not tell me of this,' turning to her sister.

'A great deal to do with it, Lady Danvers, as Mrs Winter knows. I came here because I was so glad to hear of this marriage, as permitting a renewal of our usual intercourse.' A toss of her coal-scuttle bonnet accompanied the words. 'Not that I need care,' added Mrs Maitland, provoked beyond bounds by the aristocratic calm of Lady Danvers. 'I too shall soon have to announce a marriage. But a young man like Edward is not so easily pleased.'

This was a pure invention of Mrs Maitland's, imagined on the instant, under the idea of causing the deepest chagrin to Mrs Winter by the definite certainty of the loss of Edward.

'May I ask the name of his intended?' asked Mrs Winter, with the same provoking smile. 'As I have known Edward from a boy, I may be allowed to wish him well.'

'At present we are not permitted to divulge it; the consent of a very distinguished person is required,' replied Mrs Maitland, with an air of the utmost importance. (She had it in her mind to say 'Minnie Shorne'; but the bearing of the stately Lady Danvers had taught her that a very different style of person would be required to impress *her*.)

'When all the details are arranged,' continued Mrs Maitland, spreading out the folds of her rich dress, 'I will inform you. In the meantime, good-bye. Good morning, Lady Danvers. I hope you will find Miss Escott an agreeable inmate and an appropriate companion to your daughter. I am sorry that my congratulations were premature,' and with a low curtsey to Lady Danvers, and a rather enforced shake of the hand to Mrs Winter, she found her way out of the room, under such an overwhelming sense of discomfiture, that for a long time after she never, even with Mrs Shorne, alluded to the fact of 'suicidal mania and hereditary insanity' as connected with Sophia.

'What an intolerable upstart!' exclaimed Lady Danvers, as Mrs Maitland sailed out of the room. 'Now, Amelia, you must promise me to have nothing more to do with her. The creature actually came here to insult us.'

Aunt Amelia gave an odd smile.

'That is true; but perhaps she considers there is sufficient reason, sister. I am almost certain that Edward Maitland cares very much about Sophia; his mother knows it, and for that reason he is gone away.'

Then Mrs Winter related every particular of her interview with Edward.

Lady Danvers listened attentively to all she said. One of her principal inducements in consenting to take charge of Sophia, was to relieve her sister of an irksome burden until her speedy marriage should set them free. If Sophia persisted in refusing John Bauer, there was Maitland to fall back upon ; and the two sisters, chatting together afterwards before the fire, gleaming out cheerfully from the Dutch tiles,—passed two of the happiest hours Aunt Amelia had known for years.

CHAPTER II.

WHEN the late Sir Reginald Danvers, K.C.B., left Faulds to Lady Danvers for her life, he might be said by that one act to have wiped out a great deal of the selfish ill-treatment he had inflicted on her for the last twenty years.

Situated in the charming county of Berkshire (the royal county, as it is called, because Windsor Castle, that glorious legacy from our Norman kings, lies within its limits), the house, a noble Elizabethan pile, grey with age, and chequered with coats of many-coloured lichens, stands on the summit of a high hill, commanding the whole country.

Over the principal entrance, lavishly decorated with rich carving and devices, appears in stone the peaked outline of the Prince of Wales' plume (Faulds had been built for Prince Henry, son of James I.), and underneath the arms of the Danvers, who had risen to wealth and eminence, and purchased the estate, in the time of the Georges.

Two long rows of high latticed windows, with square mullions and cyphers, break the line of mellow brick walls, and an elaborate stone cornice like richest lace-work runs in an open pattern round the roof.

It was not so much the size (for that style of house, it is not spacious), as the fineness and delicacy of the stone-work, the elegance of the embroidered cornice, the colonnade of three arches, approached by steps which formed the principal en-trance—the happy blending of the Tudor and Italian styles, and the splendour of the position which makes Faulds so remarkable.

A more perfect residence cannot be conceived. Thick hedges of cut yews, planted on delicate turf following along low walls, divide it from the park; an undulating expanse of hill and dale, studded with ancestral oaks, calmly surveying their huge shadows on the grass, a double avenue of prodigious lime-trees extending from the colonnaded entrance down the approach, and the largest and weirdest firs to be found out of Norway. To watch the rays of the setting sun reflected on their red-scored trunks, and shooting in long arrows of light, lose themselves among mimic forests of delicate ferns, knit together in labyrinths of green, under the shadow of over-arching boughs,—was a sight not easily to be forgotten.

Every separate tree might sit for its portrait as a patriarch of the woods, and graceful lines of shrubbery and plantation back up the whole.

On the south side of the house lies a broad paved platform, with an antique orangery at either end, a bowling-green beyond, and some flower borders. (I use the present tense, as Faulds still remains in all its forest beauty.) But the flowers left much to be desired. Lady Danvers, devoted to amateur farming, and visited at times by capricious fits of economy, had discontinued the expense of the flowers, once the pride of Sir Reginald's heart.

Before the grand entrance a succession of broad terraces precipitate themselves down the hill towards peaceful lawns and woodlands, a kindly site for brightest creepers and ruddiest fruits. Beyond opens the view, the finest and the most extensive to be seen in Berkshire. People used to say it was the commanding position of her house which made Lady Danvers so proud. That proud she was, there was no gainsaying ; indeed, her dignified and reserved manners might be forgiven her, when you had seen her home. But this ancestral splendour had no effect on little Jane, never so happy as when she could escape from the boundaries of the park, and run wild in the high bosky lanes, or over the wide stretches of heathy commons.

Within, unfortunately, the house had been partly modernised by the father of Sir Reginald (a change approved by Lady Danvers, who infinitely preferred the comfort of modern furniture to straight-backed chairs, and unimpressionable oak sofas, but creating intense disgust in the soul of Louis Winter, who, on the occasion of his visit, had generously offered to superintend the arrangement of the whole according to the period, a little affair out of which he estimated he should clear a small fortune). But he urged in vain ; Lady Danvers was as obdurate about her house as she was about anything else. Such as it was it pleased her, and so it should remain.

The regularity of the establishment was distracting. Gongs and bells sounded all day on various pretexts,—specially a bell, which woke every one at six o'clock A.M., when poor Jane, as has been said, was expected to turn out of bed, and betake herself to the piano in a fireless room for the practice of scales.

Of course the servants were drilled to an almost military exactness, and the really shabby meals (it was for Jane's sake, Lady Danvers said, that she did not permit an over-laden table, but the truth was, she delighted in small economies) served with the regularity of a convent. The only person who ever had dared to remonstrate was the sharp-tongued governess, rather fond of good cheer, Miss Oxley; 'a valuable person,' Lady Danvers observed, 'but distressingly forward.' She, resenting the frequent appearance of boiled mutton, had inquired if Lady Danvers' sheep produced 'nothing but legs?' a question received with such ominous symptoms of displeasure, she never ventured to intrude her remarks again.

Not only the sheep (never properly

fattened), but the management of the farm
(the money squandered on it was the
laughing-stock of her neighbours), and
Jane's education and prospects, principally
occupied Lady Danvers' thoughts. Already
a suitable *parti* had been selected for her
by her mother, or, rather, the two mothers,
for the Duchess of Upshire was quite as
anxious about securing the heiress for her
younger son, Lord Edward, as Lady
Danvers could be to bestow her on him ;
but as yet it could not be said that the
young people had fallen into the plan.
Lord Edward, as far as he dared, evinced
a decided antipathy to Jane's somewhat
rustic manners and rough bringing up, which
Jane took care to return, although severely
reprimanded by her mother, without effect.

That her daughter should seriously
oppose any desire she might happen to
express never entered into Lady Danvers'
calculation. As Sir Reginald had ruled
absolutely over her, so did she seek to
rule others.

The connection was satisfactory in all
respects. Lord Edward was heir to his
uncle, Viscount D—, and would eventually
inherit a considerable property in Wales.
If possessed of no striking characteristics,

he was his mother's pet, and Lady Danvers, indolent by nature, and accustomed to her own way, was anxious to see her daughter married before a London season had unsettled her ideas of duty, or that she herself had been put to the trouble of late hours and elaborate toilettes.

Nothing, to her mind, was so ridiculous as a love-match. What was the use of parents and guardians, but to avoid the crude idea of these selections? Besides, people living in a certain *monde* were subject to certain rules,—they must marry in their own set, and endeavour to unite both the advantages of rank and fortune. In this respect Lord Edward suited admirably. Jane's fortune was considerable when she came of age, and would suffice for the present until his uncle died.

Lady Danvers had stipulated that, in consideration of her extreme youth (those were days in which people did not marry as early as they do now), Jane should live for the present in the country,—an arrangement very agreeable to the duchess, who disliked London, and was really attached to Jane.

Altogether nothing could promise better. As far as her selfish nature allowed her, Lady Danvers really cared for her daughter ; and remembering the sufferings of her own ill-assorted union, her mind turned anxiously upon the necessity of avoiding as much as possible any chance of unhappiness to her child.

That a lady in her position should seriously occupy herself with the fate of an orphan niece introduced into her house against her will was not to be expected. But as long as Sophia gave her no trouble, she was prepared to let her stay. 'Everyone likes to have their house to themselves,' was Lady Danvers' opinion, but, as a temporary arrangement, she would bear it to please Jane. Fortunately, no one in the neighbourhood knew anything about her niece. She was a distinguished-looking girl, and could be satisfactorily accounted for as the only daughter of her brother, the late English President at H—. If further inquiries were made, the world might be informed that her mother, the daughter of a Rajah—who had lost caste by marrying Mr Escott,—died at her birth, and that she had also lost her father.

In a lofty kind of way she meditated introducing her niece to the county society as soon as her deep mourning permitted.

In the meantime, she hoped she would improve her manners, which had struck her as decidedly repellent and ill-bred.

It was just possible that her dependent position might lead her to re-consider her decision in respect to John Bauer. Lady Danvers, as a shrewd reader of character, feared, however, that with her sullen disposition this was improbable. If not, there was still Edward Maitland in the background, a much better match, in point of position, and a smile curled her well-formed lips as she thought of his mother's presumption in the yellow drawing-room at Scatlands. 'Give her a good lesson, impudent woman,' was her thought; 'my niece, indeed, not good enough for her son! Preposterous!' and then and there Lady Danvers made a note of inquiry about Edward, and perhaps of inviting him to Faulds.

.   .   .   .

The morning after their arrival, Lady Danvers called Sophia to her in the great hall, before making her daily inspection of the farmyard in company with the bailiff, an imposing personage, popularly believed to cheat her unmercifully.

'I take no part in the housekeeping myself,' she said, turning her bright diamond rings upon her fingers, 'but, I assure you, I gave most particular instructions to the housekeeper about your room. Speak to her yourself if anything is amiss.'

Sophia, with unmoved eyes, coldly thanked her.

'I want nothing,' she said; 'I have no right to express any wish.'

'Oh! as to that, I beg you will. In England, we pique ourselves upon our hospitality. When you are a little more at home,' she added, with a gracious smile, 'we must have a little talk together. I like to know the minds of those who live with me, particularly young people of your age, without experience.' Then, in her clear, authoritative voice, addressing herself to Jane, who, in a frenzy of impatience, was dragging her cousin off to see the grounds, attended by Nep, contorting his body in a series of joyous leaps and sudden plunges to celebrate her return,—'Do you not see that I am speaking to Sophia, and that it is your business to listen? I will take care you shall have a piano in your room,' she continued, 'as soon as it can be procured. I am not a musician myself, like my sister, but I wish Jane to play, and you will oblige me by encouraging any taste she has. I don't mean teaching,' she added, seeing the dark lines gather on Sophia's brow; 'Miss Oxly does that; though perhaps it might not be a bad idea,' she added, noting the rebellious look, and determined to put it down, 'and exercise you in the idea you suggested of "doing something for yourself" as a governess, I suppose, if you do not marry. I presume at present, however, that this is not needed. Perhaps,' in another tone, 'Jane has told you that I require the utmost regularity at meals, and it is my wish that you should remain with me in the evening.'

With a toss of her proud head, Sophia was about to reply that she preferred her evenings to herself, but without waiting for an answer, Lady Danvers betook herself to her own apartments, a suite of three spacious rooms on the ground-floor, the handsome furniture arranged according to the most symmetrical idea of order, but without a vestige of those artistic adornments which had made the shabby old drawing-room of Scatlands so cheerful and pleasant.

Poor Sophia! Never had she felt more humiliated in her life! ·

At least, at Scatlands she was her own mistress, and what she did, or did not do regarded as a matter of the utmost importance. The poverty of the Winters' house seemed more homelike than the cold luxury of Faulds; and, spite of the horror of that fatal letter, she had grown to love that bare bedroom of hers with the damp stains on the paper, and that high window overlooking Rosebank, where she had been visited by such bright visions. She missed the pressure of Uncle Louis's kind arms, and the sound of the silver-mounted flute in the long evenings! From the first, he had been to her a reflex of her lost father; and spite of her indignation about John Bauer, she yearned to be once more near him, and to be called 'his child.' For an instant her aching heart had gathered round her cousin; but what was Jane to her? She would only grow up to despise—perhaps to hate her.

A wave of hatred and revolt swept over her, on the very threshold of her new home, and as her eyes ranged through the sunk arches of the door, into the

spacious hall, ornamented with deers'
antlered heads and suites of ancient armour,
lances and swords hung between, with
raised stands fitted with old china, a
wild feeling came over her to fly into
those wintry glades spread out before
her (where the over-lapping boughs
formed into the semblance of an Indian
jungle), fly anywhere, rather than remain
to become the victim of the intolerable
tyranny of Lady Danvers.

'Why did I ever come?' she asked
herself, looking round with a helpless
glance. 'Why did I listen to Jane?
She is as much trampled on by the mother
as everybody else!'

.   .   .   .

In the intolerably dull evenings passed
in the octagon parlour at Faulds, oc-
cupying the space behind the oriel windows that jutted out under Prince Henry's
stone plumes,—how she missed the glowing face of Saint Sebastian, with his holy
calm, and hated the whole generation of
Danvers, looking down on her from the
panelled walls. Ladies in ruff and fur-
below; their simpering eyes all turned
one way, the powdered head of a bishop
with full sleeves of lawn; a gentleman-

at-arms in uniform, and a modern field
officer in the person of Sir Reginald,
sword in hand, charging at the head of
his regiment; Lady Danvers herself sitting opposite on a brocaded sofa, her
eyeglass brought to bear on Jane, seated
erect at the side of her governess, reading
aloud some stupid history to which she
was expected to attend.

Lady Danvers did occasionally address
an observation to her, or made inquiries
as to her health, but of her wondrous
talent for music she never spoke. This
would have involved admiration and ap-
plause, both of which she rigidly withheld,
until she was satisfied that her niece's
temper was improved.

'The girl is quite a savage,' said Lady
Danvers to herself. 'Just what was to
be expected, when poor Charles married
an Indian.'

If, by-and-by, she found her more docile
and ready to take advice, she should
change; if not, she must follow out her
own plan of 'doing something for herself.'

As yet she had never summoned Sophia
to that antique *sanctum* she called her
room. She hated talks involving discussion where she could not dictate as

she liked, and she felt intuitively that Sophia would oppose her in all she said.

In the meantime, though always scrupulously polite, she watched with growing anxiety the influence Sophia was acquiring over Jane. Some incipient indications of rebellion on the subject of Lord Edward which she attributed to her, were summarily crushed with an assurance that if the like occurred again, Sophia must leave the house; and Jane, in her devotion to her cousin, was so fearful of irritating her mother, that ever since this threat she had acquiesced in all she said.

In every household arrangements, Sophia was classed second to Jane, and this was done in so obtrusive a manner, as to infer the immeasurable distance between them in the social scale. Nurse Ludlow, an old servant who had lived there ever since Jane was born, and was permitted liberties and freedom of speech denied to everyone else,—hated her, and showed it.

'A stuck-up foreign minx, I calls her, my lady, though your honour's niece. Ill company for our Missey, I am afeerd.' And Jane and she had almost come to fisticuffs one day when she had refused to answer Sophia's bell. 'Let her call her injy blackees to wait on her, not I— No, Missey, I wont stir.'

Had Sophia been really as incapable of generous feeling as she sometimes appeared, such provocations would have resulted in a bitter hatred of her cousin ; but this was not so. In the dark English world into which destiny had led her, Jane was the one bright spot which redeemed her from despair. Alone, Jane looked up to her, spite of the change in her life. Alone she loved her ; and her child-like conviction that she could 'do no wrong' often brought a glow of pleasure into her desolate heart.

'If you only knew her, you would think her perfect,' Jane would say to Miss Oxly, in the solitude of the school-room, when, with difficulty she was dragged there from the bough of a convenient fir-tree, book in hand, Nep sprawling on the grass beneath—in answer to the remarks of that bitter-tongued lady who declared she really was astonished Lady Danvers could 'put up with Miss Escott's sulky ways.'

'Poor dear, think what a change!

Not the beggar-maid turned into a princess, but just the other way.   As for me,' in a louder voice, her clear honest eyes shining out from under her hair, ' all my life shall be devoted to her.'

'All my life,' emphatically repeated, at which Miss Oxly smiled the smile of experience, and shook her head.

(' Nasty old thing,' muttered Jane, under her breath.   'It is all jealousy,' and she turned off in a huff to master the eccentricities of the French verbs.)

Of all concerned, no one was satisfied but Jane (a little sobered at times when she recalled Lord Edward, and her mother's imperious will), otherwise skimming lightly as a bird over the surface of secret pitfalls and hidden dangers too near, and too apparent long to remain concealed.

CHAPTER III.

'COME here, Sophia, I have something to tell you,' Jane whispered to her next day, casting a careful glance towards the door (the fear of her mother never left her), 'come along.' Then, taking her by the hand, they went out, and passed down flight after flight of the old moss-grown terraces, bordered by high balustraded walls, dulled to a sad grey by the growth of centuries ; along lines of broad gravel walks, marked out by yew hedges, to a green expanse of emerald turf, where a stream ran trickling gaily over a pebbly bed, to lose itself in a magnificent bank of rhododendrons and laurels.

The country beyond, doted with a rich

growth of ancestral timber gathered round half - hidden mansions and trim - walled cottages, each with its bright garden and thriving homestead — innumerable neat hedgerows dividing the cornfields and meadows into a verdant chess-board —around the precincts of a great open common, over which the winter sun cast purple shadows on ruddy gables and chimneys.

To the right, screened in lofty woods, the lodge gates of a great hero, portioned by a grateful nation with a vast estate ; opposite on a rise a red mass among the oaks, the home of an aged statesman who, in his long life, had seen chances and changes innumerable in the political world ; in a wooded dell, literally blinded with trees, a famous novelist living beside his church, who had brought all Europe to his feet—while rising high above a wide-stretching level horizon, rolled the sea.

' Is it not charming ! ' exclaimed Jane, forgetting what she was about to try in her ever-recurring admiration of her home. ' Just the place for you, Sophia, instead of being boxed up at Scatlands. You will like England now better than India, and that is well.'

'Never!' cried Sophia, with such vehemence she made the other start. ' Do you think I can prefer night to day, or compare this horrible climate to an Indian sun ? These pigmy little woods to the green walls of a jungle, where the trunks darken the air ? The mangoes, every branch forming a fresh tree—and the tamarind, and the cocoas, higher than the temples! The sandal woods, so full of scent, they perfume the air for miles—and the lovely green roofs of bamboo ? The magnolias and the citrons ? Why, in India, we *believe* in plants and trees. To us they are *sacred.* No Hindoo would cut down the tulsi, or injure a consecrated shrub. As to the holy pipal, it may grow where it pleases, undermine temples and palaces —no one dares to touch it. And the palms, too, that are half human,—' male and female,—and refuse to live alone!'

Jane opened her eyes wide at the enumeration of all these wonders. They pained while they amazed her. How far off Sophia seemed! Still her curiosity suggested many questions, only Sophia went on.

'You would know what a tree meant

if you saw the palms. Sixty feet high,
with clusters of golden dates—and the
bananas spreading like the mangoes ; the
palmyra and sago, and the slender areca,
all growing in the compound behind the
residency.

Papa loved flowers. I dare not so much
as think of the roses and the jasmine
and the lotus swimming like white and
pink islands in the large tanks. The
sweet champak and the moon flowers ;
the birds rustling through the air, and
the death-like silence when the dust
storm comes ; the ground shaking under
a brazen sky ; the wild beasts crouching
in their lairs ; the serpents wreathed and
still ; the very elephants trembling in
the swamps, and the Indians veiling
themselves with their white head cloths
prostrated on the earth.'

For a moment Sophia seemed to lose
herself in the picture she had culled up,
and stood with widely-opened eyes bent
on the grey horizon. Then seeing the
astonishment depicted on Jane's face at
the strange burst of eloquence, so unlike
her usual silence — she paused a moment.

' You ask me to tell you about India,

I must speak the truth. I cannot prefer nettles and briars to tree-ferns and
cactus. Your miserable little black robins
and sparrows to cockatoos and parrots,
and your meagre kind of life to eastern
magnificence.

'Don't talk to me of these low flat outlines and call them views. Everything
here is so miserably minute and colourless,'
and Sophia pointed with contempt to the
glory of Jane's heart, the famous outlook
from the terraces at Faulds stretched out
before her. 'After I have looked upon
the great ghats of India, covered with
rolling mists, and the endless plains
burnt up in the hot season, but lovely
in the rains. Your pigmy churches to
the solemn temples where Zebula led
me as a little child, and prostrated herself
before the images of Vishnu and Siva,
and such a small house as Faulds to the
white palace where I lived; the great
audience hall lined with mirrors, my
father sitting on a golden throne, surrounded by guards and servants, to receive the native princes and Rajahs—
even the Nizam himself!

'In India, little cousin, there is everything—from an elephant to a firefly—so

you must not ask me to admire anything
here.   If it were only the country, I
might bear it, but the people—'

Tears of disappointment were swimming in Jane's eyes.   No; it was no
use.   Sophia would never change!   How
she hated to hear of India now.   It
seemed to sever them further and further
from all the little home interests which
were to her so dear.

'Now, Jane,' continued Sophia, satisfied with the impression she had made,
'you were going to tell me something;
what is it?   I am ready to listen.'

'I think life is very melancholy,' was
Jane's reply, all the smiles gone from
her bright face.   'Everyone is disap-
pointed.   I am sure I am.   Here are
you abusing everything in England, and
mamma is telling me that I must be
married in a year, and that our neigh-
bour, the Duchess of Upshire, is coming
here this very day to settle about it;
and I am to make myself agreeable,
mamma says, to Lord Edward, upon
pain of her displeasure.   I know
mamma.   She will give me no peace
now.'

'Why, I thought a lover was the

very thing you wished for at Scatlands.
What is Lord Edward like?' asked
Sophia, with some show of interest.

'A lover, indeed! Don't talk of it.
This one does not count. I never
could bear him. Such a little prig!
The duchess is very nice, and gives
me lovely things on my birthday; but
Lord Edward thinks himself a great
swell, and is full of airs and graces.
After all he is only two years older
than I. I told mamma I wanted to
have nothing to do with him, but to
devote myself to *you*. She laughed, and
said I was a fool. But I am no fool,'
angrily, 'and will marry no one I do
not like. I know;' breaking off, abashed
at the boldness of her words. 'It is
my duty to obey mamma; but, oh! she
could not want to make me miserable
for life! Anyway, if you were happier, dear Sophia, I could bear a great
deal.'

'Happier!' echoed Sophia. 'Happiness is not for me.'

'But, if you made it up with Mr Maitland,' urged Jane, 'and he came here.'

'No, no; impossible!' (at the sound
of his name all her wounds seemed to

bleed afresh). 'He would not come. Don't speak of it!'

'Then I must see him,' answered Jane, with a decision worthy of her mother. 'I must tell him how miserable you are. I know I could convince him. No one can speak to him of you like me. Somebody must be happy; if not I, then you.'

'Yes, little cousin; though you are English, I feel you love me,' broke from Sophia; and, in a moment, her soft arms were round Jane's neck, her lips pressed to hers, and the pent-up tears flowing fast, as she dropped her head on her cousin's shoulder, who, out of pure sympathy, cried too.

'Do not mention him,' she murmured, as she gradually grew more calm. 'You see I cannot bear it;' then, with a sudden revulsion of feeling, as she recalled the anonymous letter, and how she had been deceived, she put Jane back from her, and looked sternly into her face. 'Remember, child, I forbid you ever to mention his name again.'

But Jane was not to be put off by Sophia's changing moods (*temper*, Uncle Louis would have called it); but even to herself Jane would not admit that anything so perfect as her cousin had a fault. These were her Indian ways, she thought, which no one understood; and in her own mind she decided that she would find Maitland, and tell him how much Sophia was suffering for his sake. Why should she not? The unknown paths of life lay before her, full of possibilities and hope.

Youth readily believes in all its wishes, and young eyes look forward to vistas of novelty and hope. Later, these gradually narrow—the glitter dies out, they darken, and, alas! at last vanish altogether, as did the magic door that opened in the thick wall of the Seraglio garden before the eyes of amorous Amed, then closed, and never was to be found by him again.

Until Sophia came, no shadow had darkened the unclouded horizon of Jane's life, which lay before her like a broad, shining path, bordered by flowers, and peopled by smiling faces. But already there was a change. The gay flowers were turning into thorns, and the smiling faces wore a troubled air; the sky before so serene, was darkening with gathering clouds, and the sombre gloom that enshrouded Sophia was gathering about her head.

. . . .

Here the absurd behaviour of Nep interrupted all further talk. Rushing madly down the terraces, he greeted Jane with the most extravagant demonstrations of delight, tearing round and round her, and prostrating his large body on the ground, jumping up again with furious barks, and tearing up the hill, as fast as he had come down—as the sound of wheels became audible on the drive. The ringing of a deep-toned bell followed by the appearance of Nurse Ludlow, with difficulty balancing herself on the top of the terrace steps, crying in a shrill voice for 'Missey.'

Another furious fit of barking announced the arrival of visitors. A carriage was heard drawing up before the colonnaded porch, and the ringing of another loud bell brought forth a maid running rapidly down the terrace in search of Jane.

'Please, miss, I have been looking for you everywhere. You are to come in immediately, my lady says, to be dressed. She is very angry that you are out.'

' Do you want to lame my poor old legs for ever ?' piped out Nurse Ludlow in an irritated tone, when she caught sight of Jane coming up from below, ' a-running up and down after you like the dog ? You are to come in directly, my lady says. She is very angry as you is out.'

Upon which, without further waiting for a reply, Nurse Ludlow turned her back, and limped back into the house.

CHAPTER IV.

WHEN Jane came down in her best dress—exceeding short in the skirt and tight in the body by reason of her rapid growth, —she found Lady Danvers seated by the duchess on a gaudily-gilt sofa in the great saloon ; save for the too-modern furniture, the very beau-ideal of an Elizabethan room. The roof supported by open, painted rafters in the Italian style ; the walls hung with faded tapestry, representing the Titanic battles of Pagan gods ; at one end a carved balcony for musicians ; at the other, elaborate oak panellings surmounting a broad, open hearth. Down one side, a range of lofty recessed windows, looking towards the trimly-set bowling-green, and a paved walk, the sculptured arches of an orangery opening at either end.

At one of these windows Lord Edward was stationed, looking extremely bored, contemplating a flock of peacocks disporting themselves on the turf ; while the duchess, laden with jewellery, wherever it could be worn, and dressed in a glowing shot silken tissue,—which looked as if cut out from one of Titian's frames, —was discoursing of a bazaar to take place shortly at W—, for the benefit of a local charity, at which she was to hold the principal stall.

'The whole thing would be perfect,' she said, 'if Jane could help with flowers. She is so like a rosebud herself, she would make no end of money ! Don't you think so, Edward ?   I know you are a great admirer of Miss Danvers,'—with a significant glance at her son, who, thus appealed to, was obliged to turn round.

'Everything that Miss Danvers does must become her,' he replied with a bow, like a schoolboy repeating a lesson, 'especially if taught by Lady Danvers ;' and there was some truth in this, for as far as he had reflected on the subject at all, he could never understand how his mother's handsome friend had such a rustic daughter.

'Ah, here is the dear girl herself. How much she is grown!' exclaimed the duchess, addressing herself to Jane, advancing a little awkwardly, it must be confessed, towards her grace.

A cold salutation then passed between her and Lord Edward, a sandy-complexioned youth, with steely blue eyes, and a slight figure, dressed in the extreme height of the mode, with a cut-away coat, double waistcoat and straps to his shoes.

'I must have you too, dear Lady Danvers,' continued the duchess, placing Jane beside her. 'You look so imposing. Without you I shall never be able to manage the farmers' wives and the shopkeepers at W—. They will not dare to grumble at the prices with *you.* You have the art of making yourself obeyed.'

As this was exactly the kind of reputation Lady Danvers loved to possess, she smiled at the adroit flattery, and declared that she put herself and Jane at the discretion of her Grace. 'Jane was rather young,' she thought, to appear in public.

'Oh, no. That is all right; and if she will only make me a few pretty little trifles, as my other young friends have done, she will be the sweetest of girls. A taste for fine needlework,' added the duchess significantly — herself being a most adroit and artistic performer in the mysteries of embroidery and Berlin wool,—'is, to my mind, a mark of distinction.'

'I am so sorry,' answered Jane, reddening to the roots of her hair, 'but I cannot learn to work.'

'What!' cried her grace, laughing. 'After that beautiful gold thimble I gave you on your last birthday, and your promise to me to climb no more trees? Oh, Jane, that is a shame!'

Between shyness and confusion, Jane found it difficult to reply. To be accused of climbing trees before Lord Edward— who, in default of anything else to look at, was contemplating her with a fixed stare, and at this gave a short laugh,— was most mortifying.

'I am sorry,' she murmured, with an appealing look at her mother, leaning back, blandly indifferent, a richly embroidered handkerchief in her hand,—'but I do so love to spend my playtime out of doors; but I have my cousin here

now, who is a great musician and plays
to me, so I stay in more.'

'What cousin?' asked the duchess,
with that lively curiosity common to all
great folks. 'Have you a new inmate?'
Turning to Lady Danvers,—'There will
be music, you know, at the bazaar. Is
she pretty, and will she play?'

Now, this mention of Sophia was exactly
what Lady Danvers particularly wished to
avoid, and she showed her annoyance by
a severe look at Jane.

'An orphan niece, staying with me,' she
explained, 'the daughter of my poor
brother who died in India. In too deep
mourning at present to appear. Jane is
such an enthusiast; her whole mind is at
present wrapped up in her. By-and-by
it will be someone else.'

'Oh no, mamma, never,' put in Jane, most
anxious to explain the various reasons for
her devotion to Sophia. But a reproving
glance checked her in full career.

These were undemocratic days, when
rank enjoyed all its privileges. To assail
the House of Lords would have been
considered a crime tantamount to the
subversion of the Christian religion. No
one could bear her honours more sweetly

than the duchess,—a most gracious lady
with a pale, aristocratic face, and an un-
ruffled suavity of manner, which allowed
no passion or prejudice, no dislike or
caprice to appear, but toned all down to a
monotony of high breeding, incomprehensible to those of a lower sphere.

Beside her friend, the frigid Lady
Danvers might pass for rash and im-
pulsive. She constantly shocked her
grace by the eccentricity of her ideas,
specially on the subject of education, and
the hardy country habits in which she
had brought up Jane. But with the
peculiar obstinacy and self-opinionated-
ness which marked Lady Danvers'
character, all her gentle hints and well-
bred inuendoes on the necessity of
feminine accomplishments and lady-like
habits, were systematically disregarded.

Jane had been allowed to grow up like
the flowers of the field, 'who toiled not,
neither did they spin,' in all respects save
that of a solid system of instruction such
as is generally only given to boys. If she
was wild out of doors, she was cultivated
within ; and an eager desire to learn made
the acquirement of knowledge easy and
delightful.

The duchess had long had her eye on her as a fitting wife for her second son (an alliance into a family of the highest rank was reserved for the eldest—Lord Browndale). She really liked Jane, and looked forward with pleasure to 'forming her,' as she expressed it to the duke, and correcting those strange habits in which no one 'of birth' ought to indulge.

The duchess's mental horizon was narrow, and every idea conventional and commonplace. With no daughter of her own, just what was most attractive in Jane met with her special disapproval. Much of her mind she dared not impart to Lady Danvers, who, even from her grace, repelled criticism, and disregarded advice. But, fortunately, their ideas of an early marriage were identical. Lord Edward, young as he was, and outwardly correct, had given such indications of advanced fastness at Eton, that the whole family was alarmed. The plan of steadying him by an early marriage was considered the best cure.

'Plenty of money, and a pretty wife to spend it,' was the duke's idea. 'Not a town-bred young lady, but one with simple tastes.'

In another year they considered Jane

would be quite old enough ; and once removed to the aristocratic atmosphere of Upshire Park, her rustic habits would vanish of themselves.

As the day was warm and sunny, the duchess proposed a visit to the orangery, lying just outside the windows ; and for some time they all paced up and down the broad pavement in front, facing the expanse of the bowling-green and the balustrades.

'Such a pity,' said the duchess, sighing over the mouldering leaves of the orange and citron-trees, and the meagre show of oleanders and geraniums, 'dear Lady Danvers, you are not fonder of flowers. If you only devoted half the money you lavish on your farm, the duke is always saying, to the cultivation of your garden, you would find it cost much less, and be so much more satisfactory.'

'I daresay the duke likes to spend his money as he pleases,' was her dry answer, 'and so do I.'

Then the two ladies fell into a long conversation about Lord Browndale, and his mother's anxiety as to the consequences of a dangerous fall he had had out hunting last week.

To this Jane, demurely following behind
with Lord Edward, did not attend, or
she would have heard that 'when the
horse bolted, and threw his rider against
a tree, but for the prompt assistance of
a young man of the name of Maitland,
who, at the risk of his own life, caught
the furious animal and extricated him
from his dangerous position, Lord
Browndale most certainly would have been
killed.'

Hitherto she had followed in a silence,
which Lord Edward had only attempted
to break by observing that Faulds was a
fine old place, but that he preferred
modern houses ; when, suddenly recalling
her mother's injunction to make herself
'agreeable,' she stood still, quite awed.   It
was all very well to call Lord Edward a
dandy, and laugh at him behind his back,
but there he was, a fashionable-looking
youth, with a high opinion of himself, and
a great deal more self-possession than she
could command.   Not the kind of person
to whom she could appeal with any of her
ordinary objects of interest, such as guinea-
pigs and rabbits.   Even that redoubtable
pet Neptune himself, famed as the tor-
mentor of pigs, she felt would be a mistake.

Nep was not a well-bred dog, and would certainly be laughed at.

She thought of Sophia, and of all things she would have liked to call her down to help her ; but she knew her mother would not like it. In this dilemma, she fell back on the charms of nature. Upshire Park was a flat, ugly place, and Lord Edward *must* admire the copse.

'Will you,' said she at last, with a half-frightened air, 'take a walk with me ? There is such a pretty path I can show you in our wood. Don't you like woods ?'

'Oh yes, certainly,' answered he, brightening up; anything was better than pottering after his mamma and Lady Danvers. 'Very agreeable indeed, when there is plenty of game.'

'But you have not got a gun, and perhaps you would rather not.' Here she ventured a timid glance at his inexpressive face. 'I often go there—do come.'

With a half smile at her simplicity, he bowed, and she led the way, with terrible misgivings as to his liking it. Still, she must do something, and this seemed the best.

As they turned, the duchess gave her

an approving glance, then said something
to Lady Danvers, and they both laughed.

'You cannot imagine how I love this
place,' said Jane, leading the way, with
a sigh, as she recalled Sophia's want of
admiration for everything. 'Is it not
lovely, on a sunny day like this?'

'Very pretty,' drawled Lord Edward,
playing with his watch-chain. 'A good
country for hunting. Do you ride, Miss
Danvers? I never meet you out with the
hounds.'

'No; mamma will not let me; but I
walk a great deal. I often see you at the
meets near, and I and my dog Nep run
after the hunt on foot.'

An astonished stare met her eyes.

'You lead quite a rural life, Miss
Danvers; it must be very slow. You
should make Lady Danvers take you to
town and show you the world.'

Jane blushed crimson, conscious how
little she was initiated into the *convenances*
of life, and again wished for Sophia, who
was so dignified, and would have put him
in his place. Then, making her way by a
grassy path, under the dusky green of the
firs, their deeply-scored boles ruddy against
the sky, she traversed a belt of under-

wood on rather moist grass, and, opening a wooden gate, entered the solemn precincts of a great wood.

The silence was tomb-like; neither sound nor sun. Absolute quiet, when the winds were still; an infinite sense of rest, under the shelter of the great trunks. The trees, planted in groups and circles, formed into a succession of winter parlours, carpeted with moss and dry fir needles, and holly and yew making deep screens, into which the sun never penetrated; the maples still hanging out crimson streamers, and the silver birch casting down ringleted twigs. Now and then a bird flew down and twittered on a bare branch a few notes of its summer song, a hare raced by among the underwood, scared from his nest; and on a branch a little squirrel perched, who, at the sound of footsteps, dashed wildly away.

'Where are you going?' asked Lord Edward, looking round dismally, as he picked his way along in shiny boots, in the wake of the erratic Jane; 'don't you think a wood in winter is rather dull?'

Now, as this was a place fraught to Jane with the romance of each succeeding year, where every tree and shrub spoke to her in a language of its own, she felt inexpressibly humiliated.

'I hoped you would admire it as much as I,' was her reply, looking through the glades of majestic oaks, gathering round what had once been a kind of summer-house, now fallen into a moist decay. The tottering walls knit together by a thick tangle of ivy, and straggling cords of wild briony ; a broken, waterless pond in front, encrusted with green moss and the blackened remains of what had once been flower-beds.

'Why, ye—es,' drawled Lord Edward, giving another dismal glance round. 'In summer, it might be well enough, but,' looking at the summer-house, 'what a hideous old ruin ; why does not Lady Danvers pull it down ?'

'I did not bring you to see that,' answered Jane meekly, ashamed of the mistake she had made, 'but to admire this wild desolate spot. Do you know, before my cousin came, I spent most of my play-time here, because I like to be alone, and to spin fancies about books and stories.'

'Really !' answered he with a little laugh. 'You are very odd—quite an original,' and taking out a scented handkerchief he tried to conceal a yawn.

'I am afraid you are tired; shall we return?'

'Ah, no, not in the least. Is there much game?'

'I don't know, but I often run after the pheasants through the underwood with Nep, and the keeper makes a row; but mamma does not mind.'

'Is this all there is to be seen?' asked Lord Edward, casting a rueful glance around. 'It seems but a small place.'

Another blow to Jane, whose imagination painted it as of boundless extent.

The ultimate end of the walk was a deep, narrow dingle, between two closely-cleft banks scored with gravel and stones, over which trailed wild screens of briar and ivy, breaking through beds of yellow fern, hart's-tongue and moss.

Path there was none; a narrrow track led by deep banks of sandy earth, to a kind of low-mouthed cave, veiled by sheets of glossy creepers and trailing thorns. Every little weed and plant in festive array of winter red, wrapping the earth in a bright blanket, and, in between, a feathery vegetation of strong

rank grasses. The very stones and flints
full of colour, and here and there some
yellow buds of early primroses piercing the
dry leaves.

Never before had Jane doubted the
enchantment of this spot, which was to
reconcile Lord Edward to the dullness of
the walk. The scene she had peopled
with fairies, knights, monsters, and god-
desses, must impress him too. The cave
was the gate of hell, where Ceres watched
behind a laurel bush—the very spot where
she had called up the image Cupid. A
green bank beside it, veiled in deep folds
of wood—a trysting place for lovers—
Lorenzo and Jessica perhaps, or Rosalind
and Celia; a chain of sand-hills, dotted
with broom and mountain ash, fastnesses,
infested with fierce robbers. A trickling
streamlet, deep in cresses and mint, where
Adonis gazed on his beauty; and a little
well with a stone margin, the haunted spot
where Lucy Ashton met Ravenswood, and
vowed to break the spell.

Alas! she was fated to be undeceived!

'Why, this is nothing but an old gravel-
pit!' exclaimed Lord Edward, with un-
disguised disgust. 'The next time I have
the honour of escorting you, Miss Danvers,'

looking at his spruce coat and elaborate
striped trousers, upon which several burrs
had settled, ' I shall thank you to tell me,
that I may be prepared.'

The words were not much, but the sneer
with which they were accompanied was
unmistakable.

A feeling of womanly pride came to
Jane's relief. Was this the miserable little
lordling with a glossy hat, and neatly
buttoned gloves, who aspired to gain her
hand ? Was this the kind of wooing which
was to gain her heart ? Heart indeed !
Did he think his rank entitled him to treat
her with contempt ? Forbid it all the shades
of her favourite heroes, the Delvilles, Gran-
disons, Harry Bertrams and Lord Orvilles.
If this was a lover, she would never hear
of one again. Until now, obedient and
submissive to her mother, a very passion
of resistance stirred her breast. Let the
duchess and Lady Danvers scheme as
they would, she would never consent to be
his wife. Had not Sophia refused John
Bauer when everyone begged her not ?
She would refuse Lord Edward, though a
dragon stood at her back !

On the way home, not a word was
spoken. Lord Edward whistled, and Jane

frowned. When they entered the house, they found the duchess all smiles, drinking a dish of tea with Lady Danvers out of lovely mandarin cups, at a dainty Queen Anne table.

'Well, young people?' said she, interchanging a gratified look with Lady Danvers. (They had passed the afternoon in arranging such social details of the marriage as did not enter into the province of the lawyers.) 'You have stayed so long, we thought you had eloped. Of course you have enjoyed yourselves.'

'Not at all,' answered Jane abruptly, taking refuge behind her mother's chair, from which coign of vantage she did not stir. 'Lord Edward and I are not of the same mind.'

'Miss Danvers prefers rather rough walking,' he put in, trying to explain. 'The next time she shows me the country, I shall put on hob-nailed boots.'

At this rather rude response, her grace's charming face clouded.

'You surprise me, Edward; surely it is for you to accommodate yourself to Miss Danvers' tastes.'

To this rebuke, Lord Edward said nothing, but turned his eyes regretfully on

the diminished lustre of his boots, and
Lady Danvers, drawing Jane towards her,
whispered in her ear, ' If this is the con-
sequence of Sophia's example, I shall send
her away.'

Little more was said, but the harmony
of the meeting was troubled. The duchess
looked tired and annoyed ; Lord Edward
sullen and silent, and it was felt to be a
general relief when, at four o'clock, the out-
riders made their appearance, and the brilliant equipage drove to the door.

The duchess, who, gracious as she was,
never for an instant forgot her rank, stepped
in amid the bows and adieux of Lady
Danvers ; and Jane, then and there, standing on the broad steps under the arches
of the porch, received such a severe re-
primand from her mother, as sent her in-
doors in tears.

CHAPTER V.

'Bid me to weep, and I will weep, while I have
eyes to see ;
And having none, then will I keep a heart to mourn
for thee.'

 WEEK! only a week! Was it possible? So great was the change that it seemed a year to Sophia. And that odd dreary feeling that she was not herself at all, but the victim of some malevolent demon, who had cursed her at her birth!

Ever since that letter came, her life was done ; and so dejected was she, she cared not even to speculate as to how it might have been had she received Maitland's message. She had often courted death ; but this breaking down, this abandonment terrified her beyond words. To grow old alone! To lose that power of beauty which she had learned to appreciate as greater than that of fortune, seemed impossible to bear!

The petulant defiance she assumed at times, was often but a mask to her agonised feelings. In the presence of Lady Danvers, so haughty and composed, her pride generally kept her calm when her temper was not excited. She would bear up—she would do anything rather than show how much she suffered. With the loss of Maitland her sun had set. All her firmament was dark; colour and shape, and the fitness of things had vanished. She dreamed still, and vividly, but it was of things long gone by—yet so strangely life-like at times, that, seated at the piano alone in her own room, she would start to her feet as if his voice were speaking in her ear.

Was he already married? she asked herself, her hands resting on the keys, as she leant over the piano, drawing out acute cords in the high treble notes, in a wild, troublous measure, a burden of despair, almost of death—changing into a melody, sad as a dirge,—Did he ever think of her? A long-drawn succession of chromatic runs ending in a fantastic cadence in the minor key,—Should she ever see him again? Here insensibly her fingers wandered into the weirdest passages, with shrill shakes, fading off into inexpressible accents of unutterable woe. Then her mood changed, and a sad-phrased *ritornelle* spoke of vague hope,— floating, indefinite—but hope—with shifting pathetic changes, like phantasies in the air.

Ashamed of herself, she rose, and hurriedly shut the instrument; but no appeal to her pride could banish his image from her heart.

A very strange thing had happened to her before she left Scatlands. One afternoon, while waiting for Jane at the open green-door (it was only the second time she had left the house since her arrival), a small pale lady, closely veiled, stopped and accosted her. She was so sorry to trouble her, she said, in a hurried manner, but she had lost a little white dog. Had she seen it? 'No,' answered Sophia, surprised by her address. It had strayed, the lady said. The dearest little thing, who carried letters to the post, and waited until some one put them in the box. She

had not the heart to return home without it, and had been walking up and down
the lane. As she was standing there, she
thought she must have seen it. Did she live
near? And the small lady gave a curious
glance at Sophia, from under a shower of
light ringlets, over which fell a veil.

'Yes, I do,' answered Sophia, referring
any oddness in the lady's manner to
English ways. Then apparently forgetting
all about the little dog, she looked up at
the blank house-front, and, affecting to
read the name 'Scatlands' engraved on
the slab, under the bust of the Roman
emperor, gave a start, and turned her eyes
curiously upon her.

'Then you are Miss Escott!' she cried,
clasping both her hands. Sophia bowed.
'How glad I am! You will forgive me
for asking? But I have so longed to see
you, ever since you came!'

'I should not have thought that anyone troubled themselves about me,' was
Sophia's short rejoinder; still, so winning
was the lady's manner, she could not
feel displeased.

'On the contrary, Miss Escott. We all
know about you and pity you.'

'Pity me!' answered Sophia, a frown

gathering on her brow; 'no one has a right to do that;' yet, for all she said this, the lady's sympathy seemed sweet

'So attractive,' continued the other reflectively, fixing on her the full power of her blue eyes, 'and so ill-used.'

Sophia drew back. What could this stranger mean? Her natural sense of dignity made her feel she ought not to remain, but an invincible curiosity rooted her to the spot.

'Yes, Miss Escott, I mean what I say. You are the victim of a plot. You must forgive my frankness. I long so to help you. Do you not know that Mr Winter is a ruined man?' here the lady lowered her voice and gazed furtively up at the windows, 'and that he intends to repair his fortune by the large sum he will receive on your marriage with his • nephew? So shocking,' seeing the mute amazement depicted on Sophia's face, 'and he your guardian too! Yes, Miss Escott, I am sorry to pain you; but it is true. Every one is to be kept from the house; no one to be admitted but Mr Bauer; even Mrs Winter's oldest friends excluded. There was *another*,' and the eyes of the lady gleamed with an evil light, as she

cast them in the direction of Rosebank;
'but hearing of your engagement—'

'My engagement!' gasped Sophia,
through her parted lips (this revelation,
coming so immediately after the anonymous letter, opened to her such a vista
of mystification, that her brain reeled).
'It is not true. Stop,' cried Sophia,
stretching out her hand as the lady was
about to turn away. 'Who are you?
How do you know this? I have seen
no one. Spoken to no one. Answer
me.'

'Everyone knows it,' answered the
other, from under her curls. 'Mr Winter
took care of that.'

'Good God!' broke from Sophia. 'Is
it possible that he—' she stopped, and a
white terror overspread her face.

'Everything, my dear Miss Escott, is
possible in a little place like this,' and
the lady gave a low laugh that sounded
hard and mocking. 'You are so new to
England, you do not understand. I beg
your pardon if I have made a mistake,
but your engagement to Mr Bauer was so
formally announced.'

Again she turned to go, and again
Sophia arrested her.

'Is he married?' she asked, catching at her breath. She was so much absorbed by the thought most uppermost, she forgot to be angry with this stranger who knew so much.

'Not yet,' the shadow of a smile passing over her face. 'But soon— very soon, everything is arranged. His mother is delighted. She was terribly afraid of you. He is the most dutiful of sons; he will never marry without her consent.'

Sophia blushed scarlet under her clear olive skin. Had she fallen so low as to listen to all this? Yet, do as she would, she was so wrought up, she could not stop questioning.

'Then has he been forced?' (she almost laughed, in the bitterness of her spirit, as she asked the question. As well talk of forcing a young Hercules, as Maitland).

'Oh no, not at all,' was the answer; he only changed his mind. All gentlemen do that,' and the lady gave another little laugh.

At this moment Jane's voice was heard calling from the hall, and immedi-

ately after her light footsteps sounded
on the stone steps.

'Say nothing,' whispered the lady,
shrinking into herself. 'For God's sake,
say nothing, or you may ruin me for life;'
then adding, with a well-simulated aspect
of concern,—'Poor child! So lovely! So
abandoned! In me you have a friend.
Believe nothing Mr Maitland says. He
will never marry you. I have reason
for what I say;' and, noiseless as a
phantom, she glided into the shadows
of the lane.

Ah! could Sophia have known what
hate and vengeance shook that fragile
form! What a passion of envy lay
hid in those pale eyes, to which the
sight of her beauty but acted as a
spur. Could she but have known that,
instead of thinking of marriage with
anyone but herself, all Edward's heroism
in presence of his mother had broken
down; and that, such was his distress
at hearing nothing of her, that he had
actually brought himself to write secretly
to Miss Sterne, promising to say nothing
to his mother, if she could only tell him
where Sophia was? Miss Sterne, of
course, replying that she knew nothing

about Miss Escott, and imploring him to return.

Then he had addressed himself to Mrs Winter, entreating her to confide to him where her niece was ; but, strange to say, to this letter he had received no reply at all.

CHAPTER VI.

UNDER Jane's guidance Sophia had lost all fear of walking out alone, when that ardent young spirit was detained by lessons at home. Like her, bursting from the umbrageous monotony of the park, she wandered at will over the long flat reaches of heathy commons, by little tracks cut in the turf, where red-coated cows wandered ; droves of snow-white geese loudly protested against all passers-by, and dismal-voiced donkeys cropped the scant herbage tied to stakes. The distant rumble of a cart on a sandy road the only sound.

It was one of those days that shorten winter—soft and golden. Not a breath stirred the air, only the song of birds ;

the crackling of fallen leaves; a perfume
of bursting buds, and sweet scents from
heath and furze where the bees buzzed
among the flowers.

The sun struck warmly, and an aromatic
breath came from the massed up pine
woods.

To-day Sophia had made her way
through close set lanes, where, even
in winter, the branches joined overhead — to a mill, standing beside a
large tranquil pond. Before her was
a bridge. On one side the brawling
river, creamy from the mill wheels,
making a pleasant noise in the silence.
On the other, the miller's house, joined
on to the wooden hutch, up which
rickety stairs led to floury little rooms,
trembling all day from the power of the
machine.

Beyond lay the expanse of the widely
undulating heath, darkened by self-sown
fir trees, none the less beautiful for that;
and from the chimney of a cottage—one
of a circle that stood in front—a thin strip
of grey smoke ascended in the still air.

All was so quiet in itself and so restful
that Sophia halted, and, leaning against the
parapet of a broken bridge, gazed down at

the stream beneath. 'What is the charm of running water?' asks a friend. 'It seems to draw one's gaze and keep it. It is the movement of life in the earth,' is the answer. 'In running water one seems to feel the pulses of nature audibly beating.'

No one was about; the mill wheel whirred and droned, and the stream rushed by flecked with foam; but the fresh tracks on the gravel showed that people passed, and beyond, duck pools were collected to be crossed, with stepping-stones, over which the mud oozed.

Something in the still landscape touched Sophia. As she stood still and listened to the rural sounds, the air seemed full of hope. The fresh breeze whispered of love. Ah! why not to *her?* 'He loves you too well to despise you,' it seemed to say. 'Love him in return without measure and without stint.' 'Am I mad?' was on her lips to answer, when suddenly the sound of horses' hoofs came to her ears.

First, a red-coated rider gleamed out from under the fir-woods beyond, dashed forward and disappeared; then a black horse passed as rapidly, mounted by a groom; a white one, by a farmer in top-boots. A thin-flanked brown, leaping forwards, held in with difficulty by a lady, sawing at the reins ; then groups of three or four riders, all pell-mell. Another lady —(these lady-hunters *did* astonish Sophia, as a sight out of another planet)—this one a more quiet and graceful horse-woman, on a sorrel mare, followed by troops of boys on foot ; men with sticks,—even girls, screaming, shouting, halloing, away, away, through the breaks in the hedges ; in and out,—hurrying on towards a wide fence, which left many a rider sprawling in the mud. Some loose horses with empty saddles, galloping about in the ploughed field (notably the thin-flanked brown hunter, which had thrown the lady, around whom a little crowd gathered to set her on again ; she, not one bit the worse for her tumble, with a keen cut of her whip, gallantly taking the fence a second time and clearing it in style) ; away, away, until nothing but a line of red hovered behind a screen of hollies ; the huntsman far in the distance *too-tooing* at his horn to gather the hounds, loudly giving tongue, in the mazes of a neighbouring wood.

‘ A dratted blind county,’ one rider on a limping steed was saying to another, a

rough-coated farmer, mounted on a strong
bay cob. 'And infernally rotten hedges,'
was the answer. ' Here goes, Suky,' to
his horse, with a heavy slash of his hunting crutch on her flanks, forcing her, much
against her will, to clear the hedge,—the
sound of the hoofs dying away, as, by
degrees, all vanish helter-skelter into the
wood.

Sophia's alarm was great, specially when
she saw the lady fall ; and that she could
get up again and ride away, seemed to her
superstitious mind like the effect of magic.

She had heard of meets and covers,
hunting and foxes, and Jane had told her
not to be alarmed, as she might encounter
the hounds any day, as they always found
in the home-wood, and that it was beautiful
to see the run ; but, with her usual indifference, she had forgotten all about it, and
wandered about alone.

Infinitely to her relief, the sounds gradually died away, fainter and fainter, in an
opposite direction. Hurrying from the
road, she turned aside into a grassy lane,
in the direction of Faulds, when suddenly
the click of a rapidly advancing horse
struck on her ear, and a solitary horseman
bore down upon her.

Uttering a little scream, she threw herself on one side to let him pass, then, raising her alarmed eyes, found herself face to face with Maitland, mounted on a fiery chesnut, his young face flushed, his tall lissome figure so firmly seated on the saddle, he seemed no man at all, but part and parcel of his horse.

In the amazement of the meeting, both gazed at each other speechless; then Edward, flinging himself from the saddle, was the first to break silence.

'Good heavens, Miss Escott! What unexpected happiness to find you here?' A wild joy lighting up his face, as he endeavoured to steady his panting hunter, restive at being pulled up so abruptly, in the middle of a run.

'To what happy chance do I owe this meeting?' and, fixing on Sophia a pair of radiant eyes, he held out his hand. But from Sophia came no answering sign—as if a chill blast had passed over her, she shivered and drew back.

'I am staying with my aunt, Lady Danvers,' she forced herself to answer, shrinking from the scrutiny of his gaze. 'She lives near,—at Faulds.'

'Good heavens! And I not to know it!

Why, I am close by, at some rooms I
have taken at E—. How cruel not to tell
me when you went away. I wrote home
when I heard you were gone, but no one
answered; I could hear nothing.'

'Of me?' replied Sophia, casting on
him an indignant glance—(she is trying
to conquer the intoxication of his presence,
but in vain).

Maitland is so frankly overjoyed at finding her, that at first he has noticed nothing;
neither the iciness of her manner, nor that
she had withdrawn her hand.

'Miss Escott,—Sophia; oh, let me call
you Sophia! Speak to me.' No reply;
the dark eyelashes cast down, and the
tall figure more like a statue than a woman.
As he gazes at her, he feels how inexpressibly dear she is to him. Every fold in her
dress appeals to him, a little band of lace
at her throat comes to him as a signal of
all beauty, a coarse glove on her white
hand—something to worship.

Still, this is not the meeting he had
pictured. Forgetting his own silence,
and the strangeness of his sudden departure from Twickenham, it seemed to him
that Sophia ought intuitively to have understood his feelings, and his eager spirit is

blanked, and the wave of unutterable love arrested.

'Tell me,' and he looks anxiously into her face, 'what does this silence mean? What has happened? Are you engaged to Mr Bauer?' Again his hand seeks hers. Again no answering motion. At last her lips move. (It is wonderful she dare speak at all, with her heart beating as it does; the more she feels his power over her—the more she struggles to escape it.)

'Nothing has happened, Mr Maitland. I have nothing to do with Mr Bauer. I am amazed. By what right do you, almost the husband of another, address me as Sophia, and dare to take my hand?'

As she speaks, she turns and looks full into his clear grey eyes. To her astonishment, they flash back on her with a merry laugh.

'Who can have told you such a lie,' he cries, then, seizing her reluctant hand, he covers it with kisses, and gently draws her to him. 'My own Sophia, my queen, I am no one's husband, engaged or otherwise.' Then looking down on her with unutterable love,—' Did not your own heart tell you so? As mine whispered you cared

for no one else ? No husband—no lover
but your own. If you will have me,' he
added, trying to catch her eye. ' Married,
indeed ! To whom ?' And again he
laughed, so pleasant did the notion strike
him, as his eyes wander over each detail
of the perfect symmetry of her person,
from the stately well-poised head, to the
firm, shapely feet supporting her tall figure
so gracefully.

'Oh, my love,' drawing her, still reluctant and shrinking, closer to him, ' if you
only knew how I grieved when I left you,
you would understand how hard it was to
part ! You had my message ?'

Sophia bowed her head ; she could not
tell him she had not listened to it.

While he spoke, the same feeling steals
over her as at their first interview. His
simple, straightforward words tell home ;
there is the same glamour in his voice—
the same magnetic power in his eye—the
same power in his whole attitude ; and
that depth of unspoken homage that lifts
her into a new world.

' But you have not told me who invented
this confounded lie about my marriage.'
(Quick as thought the answer came to him,
ere the words passed his lips. This was

Miss Sterne's work. Her vengeance. How weak he had been to leave her where she could injure him.)

He dropped Sophia's hand, which vibrated at his touch, and opened his arms to fold her to his heart, when she turned on him with such a wild misery in her eyes he was fairly startled.

'How do I know that what you say is true?' she asked, in a low whisper. 'Hitherto you have always deceived me.'

'By God!' repeated Edward, 'I tell you it is a lie — a base, foundless lie! I can trace it to its source. Sophia, have you no faith in me?'

She is trembling now, and her face has turned ashy white. The moment has come that she had so passionately yearned for. The words have been spoken she had longed to hear. He was there, and he loved her; and oh! how fondly she dwells upon each feature of his comely face, — his low, square brow, the little rings of clustering curls under his hat,—the mouth full of sweetness, and that sense of power and protection which goes out from him as part of him-

self. He is there—and the whole world
seems reflected in his glance. Alone they
seem to stand like two disembodied spirits,
dissevered from all accidents of time and
space, floating in an ethereal atmosphere
all their own. But in the midst of the
wild leap of joy at finding him unchanged,
a sudden cold strikes at her heart, an
inward voice whispers,—'Too late! Too
late!' Her trust has been broken, sus-
picion has entered her soul, and every
sense within her is alive to doubt.
'Not for me! Not for me!' keeps re-
sounding in her ears like a knell. 'Not
for me!'

'Speak to me, Sophia,' a tender voice
murmurs, at which a great weakness
came over her, and she sank into
his arms. 'You love me!' he cries,
straining her to him, the hot blood of
passion rushing over him like a fiery tide.
'Spite of all you love me! Let me hear
the words from your own dear lips. Speak
to me, Sophia!' She bowed her head.
The power of utterance failed her. At
that moment the world stood still, and all
her faculties with it.

'Oh that I had only known this for
certain!' cried Maitland, pressing ardent

kisses on her bloodless lips; but even while she lies a willing burden in his arms, a sharp spasm of pain passed through him as he remembered his mother's words.

(His mother! Her name speedily roused him from the roseate trance into which Sophia's presence had wafted him. Alas! there is another world besides himself and her. A hard, cruel world of facts and realities! He must dally no longer in the paradise of his love. The time had come when he must speak.)

'Know it!' murmured Sophia with a happy sigh. 'Did you not always know it? From the first day we met? I cannot act. I am sure you knew it.' In the glance she gave him the splendour of her beauty shone out supreme! No blushing love-struck maiden, but an Eastern goddess dispensing favours to a mortal.

CHAPTER VII.

THEN, side by side, they sat upon a log of felled timber upon the grass, and Sophia told him all that had happened since they had met. The anonymous letter, at which he swore, sure of its author,—the scene in the Dragon-room at the Christmas feast — John Bauer's generous conduct—Jane's entreaties—her coming to Faulds—the haughty coldness of Lady Danvers, and her resolve to be a burden to no one and to maintain herself. Yet, even at this moment, with her lover's arm pressed round her, she said nothing of the meeting with the mysterious lady in the lane. Edward, all the time consumed with such a mad desire to clasp her to him and carry her away,

he had all the pain in the world to go
on listening.

'But, my love,' he said feverishly, anxious
that she should conclude, 'that is all past
now and gone.   In future you belong to me.
I know I can love you as no one else can.
I feel' (here his voice deepened into an im-
passioned tone, and those grave eyes of his
flashed) 'that I only can make you love me.
Yes—the first time we met, all this was plain
to me.   I never had a doubt.'   As he was
proceeding in this impetuous outburst, a
haughty curl on Sophia's lip arrested him.
His passion carried her captive, but there
was the chill of doubt.   She had been
warned, and even amid the ecstasy of
listening to him her suspicious nature was
all in arms.   Arrested in the full swing of
his eloquence, Maitland hesitated for a
moment.   Then his earnest gaze gathered
on her, as she sat stooping forwards, her
eyes fixed upon the ground, and with a
look of ineffable longing, he continued,—
'You think me presumptuous?   No.   I
am not.   I know that in whatever position
you find yourself you will command adora-
tion, for the power of it lies in yourself;
but, I think, I understand you as no one
else can, because my soul speaks as it were

to yours. Nay, I affirm that I understand you better than you understand yourself.'

With the music of his voice breathing into her ear she sat spellbound. Every sensation lulled into a charmed listening.

'Nothing can change my love while you are what I believe you to be.' This he said emphatically. As he spoke he rose. Impelled by a common force of motion she rose also. Her hand wandered over the front of her dress as if seeking to give him something to seal the bond. Her fingers struck against Zebula's death talisman. A cold chill ran through her. Was the end so near that this was to seal their union? Shaking off the sinister presentiment, she drew from her waist a flower which Jane had placed there,—a sprig of jasmine. With a strangely subdued look she held it out, the intense perfume rising up like incense between them.

'No, no,' cried Maitland, putting the flower back, 'I will accept nothing from you but yourself. All, all, every perfection, every fault, if you have any!' A dangerous fire swam in his eyes. He snatched her hand and imprinted it with burning kisses. 'You may give flowers to other men, and they may accept them;

I want nothing but yourself. From the
first moment I heard you were coming to
England, I felt that you were mine.'

'Then why did you not say so?' asked
Sophia, drawing back, a sharp intonation
in her voice which grated involuntarily on
his ear. (These sudden changes of manner
were a defect as well as a charm. The
play of varying colour on her face; the
quick protest of her features, the sudden indignation that flashed so swiftly
athwart her eyes.) 'What suffering you
would have saved me! Why did you talk
of being only a friend, and go away just
when Mrs Winter was pressing John Bauer
upon me? You left a message, you say. A
message! Oh, why did you not come yourself and speak as you do now? Why did
your mother not come?' remembering with
a pang the lady's words, 'How can I believe you?'

At his mother's name, Edward's face
flushed scarlet; he dared not meet the
questioning glance of her sombre eyes.
The embarrassment of his position was
becoming intolerable. The time had come
for explanation; as a man of honour he
could delay no more.

'I wish I could put all I have to say

in one word,' he said, with a sigh ; then drawing himself a little back, he stood before her, and in that full ringing voice which came to him in moments of emotion, he spoke with the directness that was in his nature.

'For myself, Sophia, I never had a doubt. At our first meeting I knew that, of all women, you were the one I loved. But, my darling,' seeing her look deepen and a dark terror come into her eyes, 'I cannot conceal from you that there is an obstacle. I am not alone. I have a father and a mother.'

At the word '*mother,*' a deep shade spread over her face as darkness before a storm. What the mysterious lady then had said was true : '*She was not to believe him !*' Already her heart hardened as she listened.

'My choice of a wife,' continued Edward, 'is to my parents the crisis of their lives. The advent of a daughter only less dear than I. Now I must frankly own that my mother is opposed to our marriage. I will not state her reasons ; it is needless to enter into them' (seeing that Sophia was about to speak). 'The briefness of our acquaintance justifies her in her own mind. She argues that my happiness cannot be set on one of whom I know so little. From this view all my entreaties have failed to move her.' At these ominous words Sophia's breath came hard, but she was very still. 'If I was silent—if I seemed strange, my love'—Edward was bending over her in an attitude of the most passionate earnestness—'if I did not return to you as was agreed, it was because I could not honestly say, "Sophia Escott, will you be my wife?" But no sooner had we parted than my conscience smote me. Although I left a message for you which, if delivered, you could not misunderstand, I felt I ought to have plainly told you the truth.'

'Then why go away at all?' asked Sophia, with averted eyes, the words dropping out as though forced from her. 'Is it possible'—a sombre reproach in her voice—'that you were not aware of what I felt?'

'I went because,' his face all aflame with the fear of offending her, 'I knew nothing for certain. I was told you were engaged. I had no right to urge you to refuse the wealthy Mr Bauer. I had

nothing to offer you but an indefinite
engagement. I quarrelled with my mother.
I swore I would not remain at home
until she had given her consent. Then
you went also—I knew not where. I
wrote to Mrs Winter, but no reply
reached me.'

The truth was, Jacob had impounded
the letter. Meeting his friend the post-
man over a mug of ale, to save him
trouble he had put it in his pocket, where
it still remained.

During all this time, no sign came
from Sophia. There was silence, if the
wild drumming of blood hammering in
her ears is not rather the voice of thou-
sands. Clasping her head in her hands,
she had gathered herself together, and
sat leaning forward, with downcast eyes,
immovable. Edward felt isolated and de-
pressed. Vainly did he watch for some
token by which to shape his words.
None came. Had he, indeed, put her
to too severe a test? The coldness
with which she listened startled him into
alarm.

With a weary sigh, he continued,—

'Forgive me if I have erred. I would
sooner cut off my right hand than pain

you.   Like a coward I put it off—   I
know, I know,' breaking off from what
he was about to say, 'it is presumptuous,
unreasonable to ask for such a sacrifice.
But,' and he grasped her arm so tightly
a momentary flush rose on her cheek,
'if you love me, you will have patience.
A little while—only a little.   My mother
loves me too tenderly to oppose herself
for long.   Sophia, darling, am I not dear
enough to you to accept this temporary
penance ?   Speak—   Put me out of my
pain !   Will you condescend to wait for
me ?'

How handsome he looked as he pleaded !
How manly !   How ardently he loved her !
How steadfast to what he thought right !

'Then you did not come here to meet
me ?' asked Sophia, in a low, hushed
tone.

'How could I ?   I did not know where
you were.'

'And you could go on living without
me !   Eating, drinking, talking—hunting,
even—with this upon your mind ?   You
could calmly leave me alone to suffer ?
That is not what I call love !'

Ere he replied, he paused to look at
her.   The break between her dark eye-

brows, which gave such expression to the varying phases of her face, had deepened into a hard line, the delicately-cut nostrils were dilated, the lips tightly drawn. How beautiful she was! Yet how terrible!

'This disclosure lay between us,' he hastened to reply; 'I dreaded, yet longed to speak. I was a coward, and I put it off. How might you take it? How could I dare to influence you? I have courage to speak, now that I find you alone, and here I stand to offer you my life. Believe me, my love,' his voice melting into a low softness, 'these are but petty troubles, easy to remove. Once engaged to me, you are my own. Should my mother hold out, I will appeal to my father. All I crave from you is for a little time.'

Though she stood near him, he dared not approach. How he longed to soften her by the ardour of his touch! But the mute defiance of her attitude forbade it. Repelled by a sense of wounded pride, he said no more.

Meanwhile an inexpressible conviction of wrong was rushing over Sophia like an overwhelming flood. Was she a pariah to be asked to wait? What would Zebula

say? Her father, too, who, had he
lived, would have bestowed her hand as
the choicest gift on earth! Wait! Why
wait if he loved her? He was free. She
had given him her love? The echo of
the lady's warning rang in her ears. The
sound of his mother's name hardened her
into stone. No; she would humble herself to no one, much less to her. Words
wrote themselves in fire before her eyes,
her brain reeled; but the unspoken answer came promptly,—'Never!—Sooner
die!'

'Tell me the whole truth,' she said,
intense agitation giving her an aspect of
strange composure; 'your mother refuses
to receive me; you think more of her
than of me?' As Edward was springing
forward with a violent protest, she arrested
him with her upheld hand. 'Tell me, are
you pledged to her?'

His eager look darkened. In answering this question, he could not frankly
meet her eyes.

'Pledged to wait for a time— Never,
to resign you. You have my word, that
should suffice.'

A sense of his manliness was rising
within him, that even the fascination

Sophia exercised over him could not control.

While he stood there, a subtle change passed over her, for which he was unprepared. The outward image remained, but the spirit within had fled. She rose from where she had been sitting and stretched out both her hands as if to put him back. Of all the bitter wrongs accumulated upon her, this was the worst. Such a blow!— and from his hand!

'Let me go! Let me go!' she cried, as she struggled violently to free herself from his outstretched arms. 'I cannot live to be so degraded in my own eyes. You do not know what you are doing,' wildly throwing up her arms. 'You will repent it when it is too late. I am not as other women in this cold English land. My blood is heated by another sun. You do not know—you do not know. You will break my heart. I have been so tried! I am so broken!'

Hysterical sobs choked her voice; then the overmastering pride of her nature asserted itself, and she said no more.

Shocked beyond expression, Maitland felt powerless before this storm of mistaken passion. With his whole soul longing to comfort and protect her. Something about her forbade his very touch.

'Surely, Sophia'—(he was vainly trying to catch her fierce eyes. If she would only look at him, he would magnetise her with his love),—'you cannot mean what you say? You cannot really mean to leave me? I am a living fact in your life. Part of yourself,—bound by a sacrament of love, no wrench can sever.'

No word came from Sophia in answer,— further and further she was retreating with that fixed, white face.

'I hoped,' following her with pleading hands, 'that when you understood me, you would have deigned to help. Consider, if I am true to my duty, I am true to you.'

'True!' she retorted with a bitter laugh. 'Yes! true to your mother. Break your promise. Tell her that the daughter of a long line of Eastern kings is not born to wait. I will have all or nothing.' And she turned to go. Yet, scornful as she was, and with the pride of her Oriental blood tingling in her veins, she was arrested by the haggard look on Edward's face, — the sad, inexpressible tenderness in his grey eyes.

'Is this your answer, Sophia?' he asked, following her step by step.

'It is.' She was hurrying onward, afraid to yield. 'As I give all, I will have all in return.'

' But my mother cannot be your rival.'

'I understand it so. Take me, or leave me, I will not consent to wait.'

The fury of jealousy that was working within gave her no time to think. Her attitude was superb,— standing in the centre of the lane. The yellow rays of the setting sun gathered on her glossy hair, setting her face in a bright aureole; her clear, olive skin, where the veins rose up so quickly, blanched into a deathlike hue, the proud lines of her head, the regal fall of her shoulders,— the hanging down of her fingers; the winter mists rising vague as a background;— but, harden herself as she would, her limbs trembled, and her brain whirled.

What could Edward answer? He was so amazed, so overwhelmed by the tone she was taking, for what to him seemed after all but a temporary sacrifice, speech became difficult.   He could not defend his mother's conduct, nor her mistaken devotion to himself.   Every moment made him more bitterly repent he had bound himself to her as he had done ; still, if Sophia really loved him, there was nothing which might not be set right.   Yet, how persuade her ?   Standing before her he saw nothing but her eyes lifted to his with the intensity of flames.

'Remember, Sophia, I only ask for time.   In all but the fact of marriage we are one.   I warn you—you will be brought by the force of my love never to forgive yourself for having sacrificed it.   Oh, Sophia, I alone to you can embody love !'

'Go!' she answered, looking away, unwilling to see the dire effect her resolution was causing.   (Can he bear to leave her ?   Will he not put aside all else for her sake ?   She steals a glance at him.   No ; he will not yield in what he thinks right.)

'Are we to part thus ?' he asks, watching for some sign of softening.

'Yes ; unless you break a promise you never should have made.'

'I am not to come again ?'

'Of what use ? I refuse to await your mother's pleasure.'

'What! never ?'

She bows her head. There is such a tone of agony in Edward's voice, she can hardly hold out.

'And I am to live without you ?'

'It lies in your hand;'—she speaks very low,—she is calmer now, and her face set and bloodless. 'If you can bear it, I must. I forgot—' adding quickly, in a scornful tone, 'your mother will make amends to you for me.'

Edward's soul is chaos. He is one of those men long to take resolutions, but, once made, who never change. To be forced to forego his promise, even by her, would be dastardly. Besides, he is conscious of the selfishness of her conduct. After all, it is but natural he should not desire to offend his mother.

He has turned from her. He is covering his face with his hands. He is free to go. She has dismissed him. There is nothing to keep him, yet he cannot bring himself to leave.

'Oh, if I could!' he murmurs, with a heart-wrung cry. 'If you would but take me as I am. I may seem obstinate,

severe; but oh! the folly of the woman
who plucks petal by petal of her rose
of love, and scatters it, with all its
fragrance, to the winds.'

At sight of his distress, Sophia's heart
gives a great leap.   A vision of what
their life might be at Rosebank rose in
her mind.   The cool, smooth river, the
line of sun-lit woods, the fantastic turrets
of the modern villa lapped in luxurious
ease, the sunny rays of light athwart the
lawn, the ruddy sunsets of winter through
the trees, and the cool dews of summer
lingering on the buds.   Why could she
not share them all with him?   But
doggedly she shuts the portals of her
heart, and hurries on.

'Is it possible?' he pleads, following
her.   'Without one kiss to sweeten the
long years that we must pass alone!
Think to what a solitude you condemn us
both.'

Her cruelty towards himself he must
bear, but the idea of her loneliness wrings
his heart.

'What matter?' she answers, carrying
her head high.   'It is but one life, a lost
existence.   You have given me a glimpse
of heaven.   Now it is gone!'

CHAPTER VIII.

ITH a glance of swift indignation Sophia, rushing forward,
almost fell into the arms of
Jane, running at full speed,
Nep tearing after her. Stopping to take
breath,—

'Oh, Sophia, I have been looking for
you everywhere. I am so sorry I let
you go alone; you must have been so
frightened. The hounds are in our wood,
and they have found. Did you meet
them? What did you do?' but seeing
Maitland she stops. Her eyes round
themselves with wonder, Nep also causing a diversion by the most furious
onslaught on Maitland's horse, quietly
snuffing at the grass, causing it to bound
and rear. 'Is that handsome young man

Maitland ?' asks Jane, in an excited whisper. ' How like he is to Delville.'

A few seconds have sufficed for her to take in the whole situation, with a perspicacity beyond her years. They have met, and quarrelled,—nothing at all extraordinary to this youthful reader of romances, whose varied imagination makes everything easy.

' What has he been saying to you that you look so strange ? '

The two girls are standing in the middle of the grassy way, where Sophia had halted. The nervous tension removed, which had sustained her in face of Maitland, she feels very faint, and her eyes fix themselves imploringly on Jane.

' Do not speak to me, dear,' she murmurs, her hands extended, like a blind person seeking something on which to rest ; ' I want to be alone ; ' and before Jane can prevent her, she is again rushing forward, and is out of sight, her tall figure losing itself among the breaks of fir-wood which darken the heath.

By some unknown process she cannot explain, all Jane's childish terrors and shyness vanish before this stranger, who, she decides, must be Maitland. A new

nature reveals itself within her; a veil
lifts from her eyes; in a few magical
moments, she passes the borderland
which separates girlhood from woman-
hood. Inspired by a strange confidence in the man before her, she feels
no desire to follow Sophia, whom her
instinct tells her she can serve better
by remaining. The mission she has
proposed to herself is before her—the man
she is to address is here.

Looking at him, as he stands under a
belt of trees, driving off the assaults of
Nep with his hunting crutch, and soothing
his excited horse with voice and gesture,
—she seems to behold the embodiment of
all the heroes her fancy had ever conjured
up,—from the broad-chested Perseus of
Ovid's illustrations, sailing down through
boundless space to rescue suffering Andro-
meda, to the bold figure of Thaddeus of
Warsaw,—on the title-page of a well-
thumbed romance,—sword in hand, leading
on the forlorn hope of Poland.

'You are Mr Maitland,' she says, seizing
the rebellious Nep by the collar, and ad-
ministering a slap on his shaggy hide,
which, shaking himself all over, he appears
to consider in the light of a caress.

Her fresh, young voice rouses Edward as out of an evil dream.   He looks up.

'I am,' he answers, lifting his hat.

He is so stunned by the interview with Sophia, so amazed by her abrupt departure, and the cruel persistency of her refusal, that he hardly cares to speculate who is this blooming damsel, glowing with exercise and health, who, like some woodland nymph, comes bounding over the heath.

'I am Sophia Escott's cousin,' she says, her voice trembling a little, as Maitland turns on her his grave, deep-set eyes,— 'Lady Danvers' daughter. I live with Sophia now, since she left Scatlands. You must know Faulds. There is our house,'— pointing to the lofty front of the Elizabethan mansion, backed by woods, towering over the level extent of flats, with its glistening rows of clustered windows, on which the last sun-flecks fall.

Coming after the storm of his interview with Sophia, the sweetness of this young girl, and her winning manners, affect him like a charm. Again he lifts his hat and thanks her,—he does not know for what (he cannot tell her that, by her coming, she consoles him in a moment of utmost need),—and, a little awkwardly, he explains (he is looking at her all the time, and thinking how different his future might have been if his beautiful Sophia possessed something more of her cousin's feminine address) that he was 'hunting, and, quite by chance, met Miss Escott.'

As he speaks, he unfastens his horse's bridle, which he had twisted round a bough, and is about to mount, when Jane arrests him, with a blush.

'Do, please, excuse me, Mr Maitland, but I know all Sophia's secrets. Before you told me, I guessed that it was you. I hope'—approaching him a little nearer —'you have said nothing to hurt her. She does love you so—'

Now it is Edward's turn to colour, under the battery of Jane's clear, brown eyes, as he bends down to arrange his hunter's bridle.

'It is Miss Escott herself—' he says, then stops.

How can he frame his words so as not to offend this bright young creature, who, with a frank smile, bringing out two most charming dimples about her rosy mouth, generously places herself as a mediator between him and her ?

'Do you mean to say that Sophia, out of her own free will, has left you? Why, she was dying to see you.' Then, reading with alarm the grave expression of Maitland's features, and the pained, haggard look spread over his whole face,—'But you will meet again very soon; you will come to Faulds, I am sure,'—a winning confidence is depicted in her eyes, as she glances up at him.

(Never, no, never could she have painted a hero so fitting at all points. How different to the effeminate Lord Edward!— and that sad, melancholy air makes him all the more touching. Happy Sophia, to be loved by such a man!)

'Alas!' is his reply, with a deep sigh, 'that is impossible. She forbids it.'

'Oh, don't believe her,' she cries, approaching him still nearer. 'She adores you. She will die if you quarrel. You must make allowances for her. Poor dear! I see her when she is alone. No one understands her so well as I. She loves you with her whole heart. Tell me at once what is the matter. I cannot stay. If mamma saw me talking to you, she would be very angry. I am forbidden to be alone with gentlemen. I do it for

Sophia's sake. Though '—with an arch little glance, Maitland noted as inexpressibly charming—' I do not feel the least afraid of you. Tell me at once,' she repeats, looking round, and marking how dark the evening has grown ; ' I will make it up.'

'That will be more difficult than you imagine, Miss Danvers,' is Edward's answer, with a weary sigh, as the manifold embarrassments of his position rise in his mind. 'It depends on Miss Escott, not on me.'

' But you can say at least what it is,' insists Jane. 'You think I am not to be trusted, but Sophia does.' Then, looking at Edward fixedly,—' If it is anything about Mr Bauer, it is nonsense, I assure you ; Sophia will not look at him. He is a good young man, but she does not like him. Before we left Scatlands, he went on his knees and offered her everything he possessed, if she would give him any hope, but she refused.'

All this shocks Edward beyond expression. The more Sophia has sacrificed for his sake, the more he feels the reproach of his present position. What can he say ?

At his determined silence a look of

infinite distress spreads over Jane's beaming face. The unconscious disquiet of
her feet shifting from side to side be-
trays her impatience.

'How unkind!' she mutters half to
herself. 'How unjust! My whole life
devoted to Sophia, and you will not
trust me!' Then in a louder tone, with
a touch of anger in it (it is so late, she
espies lights at a cottage door), 'I am
not a child, Mr Maitland, though you
may think so.'

'No, indeed;' and for a moment the
old sunny smile lights up his face.
'Sophia —Miss Escott is happy in such
a friend—I leave my cause in your hands.
God grant, for both our sakes, that your
words may carry more force than mine!
But,' and his voice falls, and his brow is
clouded, 'there are things of which a man
cannot speak, even to one—'

What is he going to say? Does he
know himself?

More and more this singular girl rivets
his attention. Her perfect simplicity
and womanly persistency, her devotion
to Sophia and forgetfulness of herself,
charm him into listening.

But in face of this obvious failure,

Jane's courage flies. She shrinks before
the fixedness of his earnest glance. The
quiet determination of his manner im-
presses her with a sense of awe. He
is the master, and she feels it. For the
first time, she feels bashful and hesitates,
uncertain whether to go or stay; while
Edward, roused to attention by her
earnestness, notes the grace of her half-
startled movements,—the eager curiosities
passing through her eyes—her restless,
uneasy glances, and the tell-tale working
of her little feet.

What inward tremors they betray.
What unspoken eloquence! If she dared
speak, how she would overwhelm him
with arguments!

Again he sighs and turns to go, with
the bitter thought at his heart that Sophia
Escott so little resembles her cousin.

'Good evening, Miss Danvers,' an unconscious accent of regret in his voice, as
if parting with something he would fain
have kept; 'I hope you will forgive me
if I seem reserved. The truth is, I have
not yet recovered from a blow which has
overwhelmed me.'

Her glance meets his for a moment,
then drops.

'I only want you to understand me,' she says simply.

'That I do,' returns Maitland, bowing to her as he mounts his horse, which, as it feels his pressure in the saddle, rears and jumps, greatly exciting the approval of Jane by the skill with which he quiets it.

'You will come and see us,' she says, blushing rosy red as she approaches dangerously near the legs of the excited hunter, the veins in its bright chesnut skin swelling with impatience, as it tosses its shapely head and paws the light soil.

'Pray, take care,' cries Edward, reining the horse back; 'I do not think so. I am leaving Berkshire. I cannot tell. Besides, I have not the honour of knowing Lady Danvers.'

'Oh, I will manage all that!' exclaims Jane, breaking into her habitual smiles; 'Mamma said that she should be glad to receive any one who admires my cousin.'

'That is rather a large margin,' replies Edward, laughing at the strange simplicity of this singular girl; 'so much of a woman, yet all the while such a child. I could hardly venture to intrude on so general an invitation.'

'I know mamma wanted to ask Mr Bauer, but Sophia would not hear of it,' and again her restless feet note her impatience to be gone. The light is getting so dim she ought to be at home, but she cannot bring herself to go without something more definite.

'I am greatly favoured by being put in the same category as Mr Bauer,' replies Edward, a touch of irony in his voice, which Jane does not understand.

'Will you allow me to escort you home, Miss Danvers—' to Jane, calling loudly to Nep, careering like an infuriated lion after a drove of pigs—a moment ago peaceably burrowing for acorns under an oak—one he has just caught by the ear is screeching dismally.

Now Jane would have liked nothing better than to be accompanied by this splendid cavalier—not from fear, for she loves the twilight in the woods—but from admiration, only the dread of her mother withheld her.

'No, thank you, Mr Maitland, but if you will help me to get hold of the dog—' Edward rode forward. In vain. With his red eyes burning, and his hair bristling, Nep is now prancing in the middle of the pigs, which, conscious of their collected strength, have gathered in a circle round him and prepare for fight.   A few cuts from Maitland's heavy whip and they are dispersed, and the vagrant Nep restored to obedience, his humiliated tail dropped between his legs ; the pigs, meanwhile, as if pursued by furies, charging in a body up a gap into a neighbouring hedge.

A wave of his hand and Edward is gone. Not so his image, irrevocably impressed on Jane's imagination.

'Just like Prince Charming in the Blue Bird,' she is saying to herself as she races along over the wide stretch of common at full speed.   How can Sophia send him away ; I never could.'

Unconsciously to herself all through this interview, she has been drinking to the dregs a subtle poison, that already is making itself felt.

'After all'—she reflects—'what good have I done ?   He never said he would come—nor told me what Sophia and he had quarrelled about.'   'Not to come,' seemed so sorrowful a conclusion that her glowing cheeks pale, and her lips tremble.

' He thinks I am only a child—' which is a conclusion, in view of his manifold attractions, so inexpressibly mortifying the tears rise in her eyes.

Then she begins to take herself to task for thinking more of herself than of her cousin, so that, what with Edward's handsome face, the musical tones of his voice, and the pathetic glances he cast when telling how much he had suffered, that by the time she has reached the foot of the terraces, her mind is in a state of perturbation she never knew before.

CHAPTER IX.

SLOWLY Edward Maitland rode through the grassy roads and wooded lanes out into the breaks of common,—the heather just blushing into life under the breath of spring ;—then along long dark avenues dimly shadowed in approaching night, cut in the thickness of the firs—the wind breaking overhead in sighs and moans ; lost in thought, his head bent down, his reins loose on his hunter's neck—that of itself picked its way across boggy gaps and over peaty mounds.

How different from the exhilaration of the morning start, when, with a light heart he had ridden out, confident in the ever present thought that, spite of temporary separation and harassing obstacles, his

fate and Sophia's were sealed in one.
(The recollection of John Bauer had
never troubled him at all, so certain was
he of his Sophia's love.)

Under the first shock of their interview
he determined to shut himself up in the
lonely farm-house at E——, where he rented
rooms, on the border of the wild district
which surrounds Faulds. What he most
dreaded, in his present state of mind, was
the friendly visit of Lord Brownhill, who,
full of gratitude since his accident, had been
unremitting in his invitations to Upshire
Park, and had now written to say, that the
first time he went out, he should ride over
and drag him from that 'confounded hole.'

To return home was impossible. Towards his mother, he felt at that moment
a rancour he dared not analyse. To meet
Miss Sterne, triumphant in her revenge,
would be a humiliation he could not brook.
How much or how little her fiendish jealousy had brought about the downfall of
his hopes, he cared not now to inquire.
Never could the same roof cover them
again !

His mother had written constantly
imploring him to return. She had seen
Mrs Winter and had wormed out of her

that Sophia was with Lady Danvers. But, fortunately, her knowledge of geography being limited, she had not taken in that Faulds was in Berkshire, and near to E—. But, alas! in all these letters, ill-written and almost illegible, except to him, the same bitter animosity pervaded all she said,—the same abuse, the same opposition. With pardonable maternal irreverence, she insinuated that it was nothing less than an interposition from on High that anything—even absence from her—had brought about his severance from that God-forgotten Indian girl. ' Suicidal mania and hereditary insanity ' were not mentioned, but the full sense was inferred.

No—the struggle with himself must be fought out alone ; the battle between every fixed belief, every household tradition, and the woman that he loved.

It was now that he first dimly recognised the danger of yielding off-hand to mere personal attractions ; the reaction which follows, the self-accusation,—the heart emptiness—the shattering of the idol which, sooner or later, is almost certain to ensue.

In love, as in all else, there must be

reciprocity. To a grave though passionate nature, marriage must be the corresponding balance of intellectual and physical attractions, reasonable sympathy, and kindred affinities,—else that which began in flame must soon come to end in ashes.

Sophia had led him captive by her beauty, and appealed to him by her misfortunes. He had given her credit for all those womanly graces he most prized, and had trusted to her to become, not only the joy of his own life, but the support and comfort of his parents.

But her imperious refusal to consider, or even to discuss his position, argued a headstrong will. No consideration for him had weighed with her. No arguments born of his love. Rather than yield, she had resigned him altogether. As if weary of playing the character of goddess—she had descended from her pedestal, and become as others are, reproachful, unjust, exacting. The sacred veil that shrouded her was rent in twain, the sanctity of their love made common ground.

How it had come about he could not say, but Sophia had suddenly fallen in his eyes to the level of an ordinary mortal—in some respects below it. There was the sting too,—the folly of a blind, unquestioning faith, taking for granted all it desired—setting up, as it were, the back of his pride, and bringing out in full relief her unworthy qualities.   It was failure—absolute failure.

Looking at the matter calmly in solitude, Edward could not but feel that, with all her natural dignity, and that reserve and coldness which sat on her so well, it was her physical beauty which had enthralled him.   He had fancied that the soul animating that mask of faultless features must correspond, and echo it as note to sound.

As there was nothing small or mean in her person—so he fondly argued—there could be nothing unnoble or selfish in her mind.   Had he found it so?

She had delighted his imagination—she had flattered him with her passionate attachment,—but was she the Sophia he had painted to himself?

It is true that, even at their first meeting, he had become aware that her way of looking at life was not worthy of her. That she gave way to sudden bursts of temper, and was wanting in the more feminine graces of patience and resignation,

—to a man of Edward's type so necessary in a true woman.

The ideal of his love had been wounded, but it was not a deadly wound, and her beauty and the love she bore him had skinned it over. But this time she had struck him sharply to the very core. He was writhing in the death-agony of his love. Could that love survive such a cruel blow as she had dealt him ? Could that be real which carried with it no softness—no yielding ? Was so harsh a temper in one so young what he had given her credit for ? Was she any longer the Sophia he had evoked, but rather a beautiful stranger who had crossed his path ?

Edward was very upright, very honourable. He was neither vain, nor arrogant, nor self-deceiving, but, he asked himself, how could he bring home a wife who had not the delicacy to feel for his position ? Who would rather renounce him altogether than show any regard to the wishes of his parents ? Not only would it be misery to himself, but an absolute breaking up of the quiet felicity of their home. Was this the gratitude he owed them ? They had slaved to make him wealthy, and the very coarseness which had adhered to them in

their worldly advancement, might have
been otherwise but for their simple desire
to accumulate riches for him.   .

It was a terrible and protracted struggle.
For awhile his better judgment prevailed.
He resolved never to see Sophia again.
Then came to him a picture of her de-
solateness; the desert which her own wil-
ful nature had created; and his heart
softened, and a wild longing came over
him, to breathe the air about her, to touch
her, to feel the fragrance of her breath, to
intoxicate himself in the enchantment of
her presence; and again and again he
recoiled from his determination.

For the first time in his life Edward
could not make up his mind.   One
moment his reason told him to acquiesce
in his dismissal; the next brought to
him waves of remembrance that lapped
his heart and senses in folds of blindest
ecstasy.

It was well coldly to tell himself, over
and over again, all Sophia's faults and
shortcomings.   That might be all true,
but, warm from her presence, could he
cease to love her? Abandon her to her
own hard will?—No!—a thousand times
No! Might she not have repented her

last bitter words?   Should he not give
her the opportunity to say so?   It was
cruel, — it was unmanly to expect too
much.   He hated himself for doing it; he
hated what had given occasion for it.
Every look, every grace, was fondly
remembered.   He would tread lightly on
her faults, bear delicately on her failings.

But, alas! what a dreary outlook!—
What obstinate incompatibility!   As pole
from pole was his mother to Sophia,
and he the Atlas to bear the burden of
both!

Thus his mind balanced to and fro for
some days, until he came to a kind of
truce with himself.   He would entreat
to be allowed to see Sophia; then, kneeling at her feet, with all the earnestness of
his fervid nature, he would implore her to
unsay her words.

.   .   .   .

Jane was far too conscientious to conceal from her mother any particular of her
interview with Maitland.

After her wild scamper home in the
dark,—a race, in fact, between the dog
and her,—which reduced her, with wildly
flying hair and crimson cheeks, to such
a condition of breathlessness she could

hardly articulute,—she went straight to her mother's room, expecting to be reprimanded for staying out so late.

But, with that singular indifference which marked Lady Danvers' conduct to all concerning the freedom of her outdoor life, Jane found her mother calmly engaged in finishing some letters before dinner, and perfectly ignorant that she had been out at all.

'Sit down on that stool, child,' Lady Danvers said, looking up, 'and try to get your breath.' Then, laying down her pen, the strong reflection of a lamp falling across her aquiline features, curiously scanning the face of her panting daughter, she listened to her eager tale. 'Were you alone, or was Miss Oxley with you?' she asked.

'No, mamma, only Nep. Do you think' —in a reproachful tone—'I should have spoken to him before that nasty old thing?' Lady Danvers smiled. Provided her own authority was upheld, she cared little for the ridicule cast on others. Then Jane expatiated on the perfections of Maitland, until her mother desired her to hold her tongue. 'But you would think the same, mamma, if you saw him,—I am sure you would. Why not invite him here, and judge for yourself?'

'That depends on Sophia,' answered
Lady Danvers, gravely, leaning back in
her arm-chair, the dark hangings of the
room forming a sombre background, and
turning over her rings with a slow, thought-
ful action. 'What has passed between
you and her?'

'Nothing, mamma. When I came
home, I found she had locked herself into
her room, and there she has remained
ever since. She spoke to me through
the door, and said she was ill, and could
not come down to dinner. I asked her
what I could do for her, and she answered,
—Nothing. All she wanted was to be
left alone. Oh, mamma, I feel so sorry
for her!'—and Jane turned her glistening
eyes imploringly on her mother, in the
hope that, in her superior experience, she
might suggest some solace to assuage
Sophia's woe.

But in this she was doomed to disappointment. Lady Danvers preserved
a stony silence, and that hard, inexor-
able look came into her face Jane so
dreaded. When her mother looked like
that, Jane knew she might as well address
a stone.

'This is a matter,' said she, contemplating with evident displeasure the intenseness with which Jane was watching her, 'for my sole consideration. She is under my care.'

The influence that Sophia was exercising over Jane she thoroughly disapproved. This vehemence of interest was a proof of it. It must be stopped.

'Get up, Jane, and don't be a fool,' she added, in her most chilling tones. 'What are your cousin's love affairs to you? I shall speak to her myself by-and-by, and on her answer will depend whether she remains here, or returns to my sister. Amelia has written to say that she is ready to take her back at any moment I may desire.'

'Oh, mamma!' interjected Jane, pressing forward with eager, outstretched hands. 'You would not send her away? It would kill her to go back to Scatlands. Indeed it would.' At these repeated interferences, Lady Danvers became seriously displeased, and she showed it. Drawing up her tall figure, she addressed Jane with an emphasis which boded no good to her ardent hopes.

'I must remind you that it was entirely against my judgment that I

received Sophia into my house. Her rebellious temper and obstinate self-will make
her a dangerous companion for any girl.
But I had hoped, in your good sense and
duty, not to be infected by what is so
wrong. I see I am mistaken. Ever since
Sophia came, you have sided with her in
all her caprices, and supported her in a sort
of mute opposition to me.'

'Oh, mamma!' exclaimed Jane, fixing
on her mother the light of her speaking
eyes. 'Indeed, I have not done so
knowingly. I love Sophia dearly, but I
have never encouraged her to oppose
you. Indeed, she has not attempted it,
so far as I know.'

'That is a matter of opinion,' replied
Lady Danvers coldly. 'At all events,
you identify yourself with her. As to her
visit here, it was always understood to
be but temporary. What becomes of her
ultimately will depend upon what passes
between us when I speak to her. As
to yourself, you will do well to look on
her as a warning, rather than an example.
Of course I cannot help your liking her.
I feel as you do, that her position is a
hard one. But at present that is entirely
her own fault. I have no patience with

a penniless girl who refuses an excellent marriage. None at all,' she added, tightening her large, white hands together, until the bones stood out, as she recalled how family distress had driven her in the bloom of youth to accept the hard-favoured soldier who had tyrannised over her early years. 'When Sophia came, I was well inclined towards her, but her sullen temper has disgusted me beyond bounds.'

'And what has she done?' Jane was bursting out, when the graveness of her mother's air warned her to silence.

'I am not accountable to you for my opinions. Instead of meddling in what you have no concern,—think about your own position. I am far from satisfied with your behaviour to Lord Edward. I have arranged an advantageous marriage for you while you are young, specially to prevent the possibility of such a crisis arising as in Sophia's case. I deprecate violent attachments of all kinds; they are vulgar and out of place. People living in a certain *monde* control their feelings. You must learn this. You will be received into a ducal family of the highest rank with the truest affection. Can you desire more?' With a searching glance at the crestfallen little figure standing with bent head, a fluff of curls, before her, she paused, then continued,—

'The duchess, who is really attached to you, will take my place. Lord Edward—' here she hesitated, and left her sentence unfinished. 'At the death of his uncle, Lord Duncan, he will come into a large fortune. Your behaviour to him when he came here was not what I expected.'

'And his to me, mamma?' answered Jane, plucking up a little spirit, as the manliness of Maitland rose in her mind, contrasted to the pettish insolence of the little lord. 'He was downright rude to me when we went out for a walk.'

'Nothing but boyish embarrassment provoked by yourself,' answered Lady Danvers sharply, sore at the opposition to her favourite scheme. 'He did not come up to your novel-reading notions ;— nor will any one, if you listen to the wild romances of your cousin, with her savage Buddhist notions of earth-gods and spirits. That sort of nonsense is not new to me,— my poor brother fell into it in later life.'

'But Sophia never saw Lord Edward,' argued Jane. 'I was afraid to call her down.'

'No matter, there is such a thing as mute influence,—specially with girls of your age. It is most dangerous. She ought never to have come at all,' she murmured, as if speaking to herself, Jane catching the words in blank consternation. 'I advise you,—instead of star-gazing with Mr Maitland on the heath,—to look after your own affairs. They are quite enough to occupy such a little simpleton as you. The ball at Upshire Park takes place in a few days. You know how I wish you to behave. Although I disapprove dressing up young girls, I have taken great pains with your ball dress, to please the duchess.' (She had directed Miss Oxley to do so, but for herself had done nothing.) 'It is ordered in London; white Brussels lace on white satin, with knots of roses and lilies.'

'Oh, mamma!' exclaimed Jane, clapping her hands in an ecstasy of delight. 'White satin! Why, it is like a bride.'

'Well, and if it is, is it not appropriate? A bride, or shortly to become one. It is all the same.' And again she gave one of those searching glances which seemed to read into the recesses of Jane's inmost soul.

' But, mamma,' she murmured, her brain turning as in a maze,—' surely you will give me time ? You will not force me ?' Her eyes filled with tears,—one big drop over-brimming finding its way down her cheek, and melting into the dimples about her lips.

'You are my only child,' was the answer. ' Whatever is my duty towards you, will be done, you may be sure;' then, with a softened voice, ' Jane, I need not tell you, you are all the world to me.' As she spoke, Lady Danvers rose, and drawing her to her, gave her one of those rare kisses she so seldom bestowed, then signing for her to go,—' I must finish these letters before dinner,' pointing to a heap of papers on the table, ' and the first bell has rung.'

. . . .

This conversation left Jane in such a state of mental confusion, she felt as if she should never be able to think clearly again. If Sophia still insisted in refusing Maitland, whom would he marry ? It was her duty to reconcile them, that was clear. Her duty and her pleasure. And then ? And then ? Would he care to remember the little peacemaker who had bridged the abyss Sophia's will had sunk between them? Would he thank her? And Sophia? In the fulness of her girlish fondness she had said, she could 'bear anything if Sophia were happy.' Those words came to her now with a sharp pang. Why should Sophia's union with Maitland be anything but a matter of rejoicing? Had she not willingly dedicated herself to her?

. . . .

She was standing under the carved niches in the great hall where the shadows had gathered at the foot of the broad staircase, losing itself in gloom among folds of huge picture frames and tapestry. The light still flickered on the big latticed casements, and a star or two gleamed in the frosty sky.

A dull pain came to her as she stood there; a strange desolate longing! How little value she was to any one! Sophia had Maitland. Whom had she? Why she began to cry she could not have told, but she did, bitterly for a few minutes. A great solitude seemed gathering round her. No one in whom to confide. So much to tell, yet when she came to consider it, no one to listen!

Step by step she ascended the oak staircase to her room. If she could only have gone to Sophia! If her mother were less hard! The whole world seemed turned against her. Yet of what had she to complain? Then, as if her rapid steps would free her from herself, she rushed down the ancient gallery which traversed the whole of the upper storey to an oriel window at the end, and sank sobbing on a bench, her hands pressed to her head.

'If life was to be so difficult, what could she do?'

CHAPTER X.

SPRING had come in early April.
The west winds blew softly,
laden with vernal scents, clouds
roll across a blue sky; a boun-
teous sunshine plays on the outlines of
the great trees, and on the underwood
of coppice just reddening into bud. The
grassy glades and verdant alleys winding
along the chase, shine in a fresh greenness.
The little brooks take a deeper tint over
beds of dark moss and reeds—the lazy
river Loddon overflows with abundant rain,
and nosegays form themselves on its grassy
brink of yellow flags and purple grasses,
bee orchids and stitchwort, in a matching
of colour no mortal could achieve. Gnats
dance in the air, the song of the thrush and
the blackbird echoes in the woods. The

young lambs bleat in the meadows,
and the frogs chirrup under the damp
banks.

Already the honeysuckles show signs
of life ; the sankle and dog mercury are
thrusting up curled leaves ; the white
buds of the wild violets gleam in the
warm uplands under the fallen leaves ;
the hawthorn in the hedges puts forth
green shoots ; primroses tuft themselves
on the dark soil of the shelving lanes ;
withys canopy themselves with fluffy
palms, and the dark netwwork of nut
branches are tangled with pink.

Though the year is young, already the
days are lengthening,—the mornings open
with a gentle breeze ; the evenings at
sunset glow with a yellow light, and the
sunbeams have power, for the equinox is
near.

Marvellous is the change. Everything
in field and woodland prospers and smells
sweet ; the intoxication of spring is in the
air. The young corn shoots upwards in
the furrows in delicate green sheaths ; the
bees go from crocus to snowdrop with the
voice of spring ; the plum and the apricot
whiten on the garden walls ; the cherry
in the hedge, and the homely wallflowers

and stocks in the borders wake up as with a kiss.

.   .   .   .

To this general rejoicing the heart of Jane responds. Sad as she went to bed last night, and haunted even in her sleep by the desire to comfort Sophia, the morning brings to her fresh ebbs of joy. Seen under this medium how sweet and entrancing life appears. Surely no one can be unhappy in a world so fair!

No hour is too early for her to rise, and race over the gravel walk, and up and down the flights of steps connecting the terraces, the keen morning air puffing in her face. There is a magnetic ecstasy in the mere act of motion as she bounds along on those impatient feet of hers. The dog leaping after her, breaking the morning silence with his jocund barks.

(Never at any time a dog of judgment, at this moment Nep has altogether lost his head. Dashing at her spasmodically, his big paws have torn her dress, wildly barking the while at the havoc he has made. She caring but little about it, stopping to knot up the rent, then running after him at frantic speed towards a drove of geese, splashing in a muddy pond, their

long projecting necks and fluttering wings
open to engulph them.   But what matter?
Both Nep and his mistress strung up to
pleasure's highest pitch bound on.

A wild chase succeeds across the bowling-green in which the dog beats, then with
a miraculous power of vision, and giving
loud tongue, he circles at full speed round
an ash where he spies a squirrel perched
upon a bough.

At last, panting and out of breath, Jane
visits her pets—gravely discoursing to the
cow-boy, who stands by, leaning on his fork
with stupid eyes and listens, as to a young
oracle, regarding the food to be dispensed
to a litter of pigs, whose savage-minded
mamma is suspected of infanticide.

The spaniel puppies nestling among the
fresh stable straw in a basket are engross-
ing, and Muff, their young mother (inclined
to snap) has nevertheless to be decorated
with a blue ribbon about her neck; Nep,
with big flaming eyes, looking on.   The
intense jealousy which rages in his breast
assuaged by a fussy bark.   Round and
round, Muff intent on her maternal duties,
he ambles, snuffing at her condescendingly
as at a troublesome person fortunately removed out of his path.   A dog's thoughts

cannot be read.   Perhaps Nep flatters himself her absence may be permanent, and he proudly kicks with his hind legs morsels of straw into her face.

Then a young calf has to be visited, tied to a stake in a nook of unkept shrubbery behind the stable ; the mother-cow, fierce in her injured maternity, separated by an ill-kept fence, at which she butts persever-ingly, the calf replying in angry moans.

As to the horses, Jane would have lived in the stable if she dared,—caring not one whit for risk of kicks or bites in entering the stalls,—but that was a pleasure firmly forbidden by her mother, though she did now and then edge herself in with a guilty glance at the groom, touching his cap with a deprecatory air,—her hands full of sugar for a favourite mare, which, whinnying, welcomes her and turns its head.

Then, with her hat thrown back, and hanging on her back, her soft hair flowing dishevelled about her, and her torn dress knotted up like a kilt, she is kneeling on the damp stones of the ancient orangery, with its stone gargoyles and fretted roof, gathering every flower she can find for Sophia.   Nep, not satisfied at the prospect, seated on his haunches wagging his wiry

tail, and with intense doggish eyes asking
as plainly as language can say it, 'Take
me a walk.' 'No, Nep, no. Impossible
to-day,' answers Jane, patting his eager
nose ; 'you must take nothing for granted,'
to which he responds by a depression of
his tail, lifting up his head, and giving a
little whine.

Then the breakfast-bell rings, and Jane,
aghast at the appearance of her frock, with
one bound rushes into the house to con-
front Miss Oxley, and confess to having
gone out and forgotten to practise her
scales.

.   .   .   .

'But he is beautiful,' cries Jane, bursting into Sophia's room an hour later, her
flowers in her hand. 'Like a Greek god!
How can you find it in your heart to
quarrel with him ? '

Sophia starting as if a bullet had struck
her ; and, half rising, cast on her so strange
a glance, it seemed as if some evil soul
had passed into her eyes. She was lying
stretched on a couch where she had flung
herself last night,—too bewildered fully
to realise the sudden calamity which had
befallen her.

It was a pretty room, with high latticed

windows, through which the sun poured, spite of the still drawn curtains, which flung a crimson glow upon the high, sable-draped bed and sombre furniture—looking out on the turfy bowling-green, set with quaint borders of boxwood and yew, and beyond a sunk fence the majestic outline of the avenues of ancestral firs, lifting their tawny mastheads to the sky.

'But, Sophia,' cried Jane, casting herself down on the floor beside her, and grasping her cold hand, will you not speak to me, your little Jane?'

Something in Jane's words broke the spell of her suffering; she rose, and sat up, then with a low and exceedingly bitter cry, stretched out her hands.

'Beautiful — yes!' she whispered. 'And I did love him! He might have known it.'

She had thrown a white dressing-gown round her when she first returned last night, and it clung to her—to Jane's fanciful imagination—like the folds of a shroud. She shuddered as she looked at her. Surely nothing living could be so ashy as the white misery of her face,—her eyes heavy and dark under the lids, her lips dry and colourless, the thick folds of

her long hair twisted in and out about her
head intensifying her pallor.

' But I am come to make it up,' eagerly
cried Jane, all the warmth and tenderness
of her nature strung up to an intenseness
of sympathy. ' He asked me, Maitland
did. · He trusted me. Everything shall be
put right if you will only tell me the cause.
He asked me himself—I come from him.'

' No, no !' exclaimed Sophia abruptly,
' that cannot be. He never saw you before ; he could say nothing to you he did
not to me. You dare not come in between
him and me !'

She rose and tried to stand, but would
have fallen if Jane had not put her arms
round her, — and half-supported, half-led
her to a low chair before the fire, where
her head dropped wearily against a pile
of cushions at the back, Jane hanging over
her in a passion of tenderness, chafing her
icy fingers, which she repeatedly raised to
her lips.

' I am better now,' said Sophia faintly,
trying to disengage herself from Jane.
' Thank you. Only restless for want of
sleep. Forgive me for making a scene.
I hate it. I am very tired, and my head
feels so strange.'

There was an underlying reproach in Sophia's manner, a nascent sense of injury, which wounded the ardent girl to the heart's core. When she burst into the room with the flowers, which lay scattered on the floor, she would willingly have offered her life's blood for Sophia. Now, without knowing why, she felt put aside and ill at ease.

'But you will surely tell me why you fell out,' pleaded Jane, rallying gallantly to the sense of her duty.

'Ah, then, he did not show you *that* amount of confidence when he made you his deputy,' was Sophia's ambiguous answer, lifting her weary eyes with a sudden flash, as she sat languidly swaying herself to and fro before the fire—which dazzled and perplexed Jane. 'Do you not think I had better follow his example? Of what use is it to discuss the past?'

'Oh, do not play with me like this,' cried Jane, coming very close, her little dimpled mouth quivering painfully. 'It is too hard,' and she clasped her hands. 'Why are you so changed? What have I done? Why may I not help you?'

'No one can help me,' answered Sophia, in a low tone. 'They may harm me, but cannot help me.   The good spirits have left me, and so will you.'

'Never, never,' cried Jane, in a wild paroxysm of affection, folding her in her arms.   'Have I not sworn that your happiness is mine ?   If you would only speak. There must be some misunderstanding— some mistake—he is so good, so noble! Such a king among men!   Do you know, Sophia, as he stood there in the Red Lane, shading his face that I might not see how he suffered, and spoke in that sweet voice, I thought that, of all living creatures, you had won the handsomest and the best!   And he was not at all offended either at what I said, and *almost* told me everything.   I promised for you, Sophia, indeed I did.   I took upon myself to make it up.   I asked him to come here.'

To all this Sophia listened with downcast head.

'Nothing can be more easy,' she said, with affected calm.   'You seem to have become so well acquainted with him already, why refer to me ? '

'But, Sophia, how strange you are!' exclaimed Jane, not in the least understanding the jealous passion that was working at her heart.   'Surely you would see him when he comes only for you? What am I but your double—your little friend? I want to act for both. Are you and he not one?'

'No,' she answered, as, sunk in her own dark thoughts, she rose, and paced up and down the room, her arms folded over her heart to still and crush its beating, and jerking out her words, as if each phrase was forced from her. 'Not if you have gifted him with all the perfections in the world, which I have no doubt he reciprocates. You have all I want: riches, position, prosperity, and friends.' (With what scathing bitterness it came over her,—his hardness, his worldliness. Would his mother have stood between them, had she not lost her father, and become dependent and poor? At Faulds she had come to understand more of English customs, and had heard much that to her understanding seemed mean and sordid. The image of Jane's fresh young face, and the consciousness that she possessed all which had once been hers, added fuel to the flame of her anger.)

'Sophia, you do me a great wrong,' was Jane's answer, immeasurably shocked as the meaning of Sophia's words shot through her mind, the flush on her face deepening to a swift, indignant scarlet. ' If ever one was true to another, I am so to you.'

'True, yes, I believe it, until you saw *him*. Can you look me in the face, and deny that you love him ?' She paused in her weary walk, and fixed her deep eyes full on the trembling girl—her face white as marble,—even her lips bloodless. No look of life was in her.

Jane covered her face with her hands. Her conscience smote her before the fixedness of those glassy orbs. Never to herself had she owned it. Now face to face with Sophia, she found not a word to say.

' I know it,' murmured Sophia, resuming her pacing. 'All gone,—all turned against me,—even my little Jane.'

'Sophia, Sophia !' her honest eyes fixed fearlessly on the other's face. Then, springing up and seizing her in a wild embrace, her lips pressed to the other's poor cold cheeks,—' No reproaches shall part us. I never said it. You frighten me. I don't know what I mean. I *do* admire Maitland, but it is for you— Tell me, only tell me, what I can do.

I feel as if my love for you could move mountains.'

'Perhaps,' was the cold answer, 'but it will not take out that which is growing in your heart. I saw it when you entered,— he has cast his spell upon you.'

Jane's spirit sank within her; her eager arms fell to her side. Her whole soul revolted against the falseness of the charge. By no word or look had she justified Sophia's accusation. *But was it true?* Painfully and vividly the whole scene of the meeting rose before her. Maitland's tall, manly figure, erect against the evening sky, his gracious face as he reasoned,— the passion of his words. What could she have done more? Then, with a terrified start, she remembered the warning of her mother, not to interfere; and the distracting fear came over her that Sophia would repulse Maitland, under the impression of this fatal jealousy. At this thought all her tenderness welled up afresh.

'Darling Sophia!' she cried, 'I am all for you. I do not think of myself. Whether I care for Maitland or not, does not matter. You must be reconciled. If you hold out, I do not know what will happen. You love him, why let some foolish quarrel part you? If it were a great thing, I should have known it. Oh, yield, do yield!'

The two girls stood opposite each other—Jane, slender, and beaming as a fresh-blown rose, her undulating figure full of childish grace,—her brown, supplicating eyes rounded, — her little hands stretched out in an agony of entreaty, her whole frame vibrating like some delicate human instrument, whose cords awaited the master-touch. Sophia, with the majesty of a dethroned queen, trembling with passion —her Indian blood on fire. The vagrant spirit that was in her bursting into flame. With a wild gesture she rushed forward —as if she would sweep Jane from the earth.

'And you can stand there and own that you love him, and offer your treacherous help! For shame, for shame! Begone out of my sight!' And in a whirlwind of passion she drove her from the room.

CHAPTER XI.

AN hour later Sophia was dressed, and seated before Lady Danvers in one of that long, low suite of rooms adjoining the hall, into which no one ever penetrated without a special summons.

'I have sent for you,' said that august lady, seated at her desk, her handsome face immovable in its perfect composure, 'to speak on a subject which, I fear, I have neglected too long. Sit down, my dear, and try to listen to what I have to say.'

Something about Sophia's entrance, some little trick of face or carriage,—the dull expression of her clouded eyes, as she turned them on her aunt, with a scared, weary look, as of some animal brought to bay—forcibly brought before

Lady Danvers the image of her dead brother. That was the look he must have worn when, overwhelmed by ruin and remorse, he had lifted his hand to take away his life. And Sophia was in trouble, and had taken refuge in her house, and if she would change that sullen temper and obey her, she might take her daughter's place.

Under the pressure of these thoughts her aspect softened, her voice took a tone of unusual gentleness, and the manner in which she offered Sophia a chair, was more cordial than anything that had passed between them since she came to Faulds.

' I hear from Jane that you have met Mr Maitland,—accidentally, I believe?' Sophia bent her head without speaking. At his name, thus openly pronounced, a pang struck through her. This putting them together made her realise the more how much they were apart.

' Surely, Sophia, all this was needless. Had you chosen to acquaint me with your mutual feelings, I should have been happy to invite him here. I had heard of him from my sister, but I did not know you were engaged.'

Sophia was so weakened by the weary sorrow of the past night, that the soft gentleness of Lady Danvers made the tears rush into her eyes. She turned away her head to brush them off.

'We are not engaged,' was her answer, feeling as at the scarifying of a bleeding wound. 'We never were. Now we are parted. We shall never meet again.'

'And why?' asked Lady Danvers, in an irritated tone. At least, she felt, this penniless niece she pitied might have deferred to her before deciding,—asked her counsel,—implored her help. 'Why?'

'That,' answered Sophia, 'I must decline to tell. There are many reasons that part us; but one is a condition to which I cannot accede.' Her voice sounded thick, and her words came slow. This open discussion of her inmost soul was agony to her. Hardly could she contain herself sufficiently not to rise and go.

'Then you mean to say,' continued Lady Danvers, with rising anger,—leaning back in her chair, and bringing the battery of her clear hard eyes to bear full on Sophia, —'that as you dismissed Mr Bauer capriciously at Scatlands, spite of all warning and advice, you are doing the same now? Do you remember what I then gave as my opinion of the conduct of a young woman dependent on her friends, who persisted in refusing an advantageous marriage? How much more now, when, as I hear, you love Mr Maitland.'

'Love him!' echoed Sophia, waiting a moment before she replied, catching her breath, in a silent spasm, which made her press her hand to her side, her ears drumming with a sound like the peal of an organ,—'Yes, that is why I will not marry him.'

This speech but tended to increase Lady Danvers' indignation. Here was this impossible girl, towards whom the common blood flowing in their veins had warmed, for whose desolate position she had, but a moment before, felt real compassion— putting her advice aside, as if it did not concern her; she, whom she had taken into her house, and would have married with the *éclat* which became her niece, and started in the world, dowered with her beauty,—the only creditable relation she had alive; here was this girl, despising her, and rushing on her fate, deep down into that family abyss of misery and distress

into which one after the other of her kin
had fallen.   It was intolerable, exasperat-
ing !   She must be mad, she thought, as
she turned a haughty glance at her, which
brought a flush of colour into Sophia's face,
dying away again into the same marble hue.

'Have you considered what this will
lead to ?' she asked, with frigid courtesy.

'I have,' answered Sophia, firmly; 'and
I am prepared.'

'If, for the second time, you refuse to
marry an excellent man who loves you, you
cannot remain here.   I would not countenance my own daughter in such a course.'

'I am prepared to go,' answered Sophia,
with a natural dignity so true, even the
anger of Lady Danvers faded before it, as
a thing of nought.

'What! penniless ?'

'Yes.'

'And alone ?'

'Yes, alone !   Whither I go, no one can
follow me.'

'Have you any money?   What are your
plans ?'

'Permit me,' said Sophia, rising, 'after
this interview, to think them over.   As
yet, I am unprepared.'

'Do you need help ?' Sophia's lips

moved, but no words came.   ' As my
brother's child, remember, whatever you
are in need of, I will supply most willingly.
If you desire to return to Scatlands, my
sister will receive you.   If you wish to
earn a living— But, let me hope,' she said,
bringing her speech into a kinder tone,
' that all this is useless.   A mere display
of temper,—and that you will be better
advised than, with your tender nurture, to
go out alone into the world.   A step which
my brother, your father, would have disapproved beyond all words.   It is in his
name I warn you.   Poor Charles !'

At her father's name Sophia started,
and, overcome by silent suffering, clasped
her hands.   ' I cannot change,' she murmured ; ' it is too late.'   Then, mastering
herself by a great effort, ' I thank you,
Lady Danvers,' she said, more calmly.
' You mean well.   Perhaps, had we spoken
sooner all might have changed, but my
mind is made up now, and I will go.'

' Not hurriedly, or angrily,' said her
aunt, taking her hand, impressed by the
majestic composure that marked Sophia's
words.   Had she complained or protested,
cried or used hard words, Lady Danvers would have dismissed her without a

thought; but this measured speech, and calm oriental dignity, found such an echo in her own proud soul, her heart yearned towards her as it had never done before.

'Think it all over,' she said, laying her large white hand on Sophia's arm. 'Decide at leisure—no one presses you. Think of what you are resigning in refusing such a man as Mr Maitland. I hear nothing but good of him. Do nothing in a hurry. Jane,' she continued, with a smile, which found no response in Sophia's colourless face, 'will miss you greatly. Remember you need not go.'

But she listened without understanding; her soul was far away, in that sunlit land where life had been all joy, where her father had lapped her in arms of ineffable fondness, and Zebula hovered round her to ward the very winds of heaven from rudely touching her.

So worn was she—so broken by want of rest—so desolate in her loneliness, so hopeless,—even her little Jane turned false, and gone against her,—that, fumbling as one blind, she found the door and turned the handle.

'Sophia, you are suffering,' said Lady Danvers, rising and following her. 'Be wise, my dear, reconcile yourself with Maitland, and stay with me.'

' Never,' cried Sophia, drawing herself up to her full height, her fierce black eyes flashing, and the long eastern eyebrows raised, on the tawny richness of her brow,—and with a quick step she closed the door.

Slowly she passed through the long suite of Tudor rooms—the walls alight with a sort of dull magnificence, the brocades and the velvets, the carvings and the marbles calling out for a gorgeous company which was not there —into a long stone gallery narrow and vaulted — here and there a quaint old deep-set casement — breaking the wall. At the end a disused chapel, mouldy and dusty, with an half-open door. Here she took refuge. It was so still and calm, the huge arched rafters making a kind of throne of the disused altar, where tufts of faded natural flowers bloomed woefully in the shadows. Seated on the remnants of what had once been a carved stall blackened with neglect and age (for many years the inhabitants of Faulds have been staunch Protestants), conflicting thoughts crowded into her brain. It was

all over then.   Again 'she was adrift.'
She must go—what matter?   One word
would end it.   Never could she bring herself to speak that word.   He was no true
man to ask it.

Alas! was there no spirit among those
Zebula evoked that would help her in her
need? Zebula! As the name came to her the
air seemed to ring with the curses she would
call down on those who ill-used her child!
To prefer the vulgar pride of his mother
to the treasure of her love! What was she
to him compared with her ?   And to divide
himself from her by a promise! Alas! This
was not what she had pictured! A cold,
poor heart! Duty! Had he no duty to her?

At the thought of her loneliness blank
misery overcame her.   She turned her
throbbing head towards the wall.

'Why is he so cruel as to sacrifice me
to another? Rather than submit to the
insults of his family I would willingly die!'

Die! Had not Zebula told her to die if
the world was too hard? Had she not
furnished her with the swift means ? How
often she had pressed that poison to her
breast, as a miser handles his treasure!
Die! and know that her spirit would return to sojourn in a glorious day among

her people, far from this land of gloom and anguish. Die! And entomb her love for ever, in a sepulchre of night—as a thing born—but to perish; an unripe fruit—nipped ere its prime,—never to be gathered by that beloved hand—nor consecrated by the avowal of a kindred soul!

Then the charm of his voice came to her in its rich, deep tones. She seemed to hear him as he spoke; the troubled brain could bear no more, the rhapsody was too near death. Life, hope, ruin, and love deeper than the grave, overcame her, and like a beautiful ghost that wanders under the pale precincts of the moon, she sank down inanimate on the cold floor, as if life had already snapped asunder.

.   .   .   .

How long she lay there she knew not. When she rose up, cold and bewildered, she found herself in the quiet hall, under the armour, and the trophies of shields and crossed lances. Jane, who had been vainly searching for her, standing before her.

'Sophia,' she whispered, not daring to approach too near, 'you must forgive me.' Then, raising her voice, 'You must, or I will not go to the ball. I am waiting here to tell mamma so. If you will not trust me as you used to do, I will not stir. I don't care for the duke, nor the duchess, and I hate Lord Edward with all my heart; whatever mamma may say, no one shall move me unless we are friends.'

There was such a plaintiveness in Jane's appeal, such a longing fondness in the way she held out her hands, that Sophia paused, as she was turning away and raised her eyes.

' No, no!' she said, speaking in a low voice, out of which all expression had vanished. It can never be the same. Let us not speak of it. Go to your ball, child, and enjoy yourself. I shall not blame you. You'—and a quick glance flashed across the ashy misery of her face—'are of the future—I am of the past. Each follows her own fate.'

And with a deep sigh she turned and slowly mounted the broad steps of the oak staircase, without one glance at the slight little figure sunk helpless on a chair, convulsed by passionate sobs, the full rolling tears over-flowing her fingers as she pressed them to her eyes.

As to the ball, Jane knew she must go, and that any reluctance would only make

matters worse. This caused her to sob
the more. Her first ball, and to be so
wretched! Oh! it was too hard! But
even if she could have stayed at home,
Sophia was angry and would not care.
Although, in the truthfulness of her nature,
Jane did not altogether acquit herself, and
a tell-tale blush dyed her rosy-red as she
thought of Sophia's accusation, yet she felt
she had done nothing to deserve such hard
and overwhelming reproaches. Even in
sleep the desire to help her had haunted
her very dreams—and now they had parted
in anger.

'It was more than she could bear,' she
kept repeating to herself, and another and
another sob shook her where she sat—
the sobs longer between indeed, but very
bitter. For the first time in her life she
found herself doubted.

Not one whit less did she love Sophia,
nor cease to grieve over the breach, but
somehow, little by little, the recollection
of that immaculate white dress lying on
her bed—the satin so pure and sheeny, the
lace so lovely—came into her mind.

This very evening was the ball, and as
one by one the tears dried on her cheeks,
she began seriously to turn over the gravity

of the necessary preparations, among which a new pair of "supports" (to her simple mind a prison of iron, invented by Philistines) took a prominent place ; also the difficulty attending putting on the lovely lace body, which was so tight upon her slight person that three successive laces had broken in the operation of trying it on. Then there were the shoes with the little cockades, and an embroidered handkerchief as fine as a zephyr, and some artificial roses for her hair more beautiful than any real ones.

'Remember!' Lady Danvers had said to her, 'not to tread on your dress,' a catastrophe which struck Jane as so very terrible she could not glance at the possibility without a shudder ; 'and you must hold in your hand a fan and a bouquet' (at which she expostulated). 'Oh, nonsense! You must do it, every-one does. The duchess has sent over some hot-house flowers, and I will look you out a fan.'

Vainly did Jane plead her awkwardness and her desire to keep her hands free.

'Impossible!' cried her mother, impa-tiently, pointing to the flowers. 'A fan and a bouquet are indispensable to every young lady. Before we start I will place them in your hand.'

But no happiness is without alloy. The long-looked-for day had come, and she was wretched, yes,—another sob,—*wretched.* Yet spasms of pleasure would keep passing through her like electric shocks, notwithstanding the thought of Sophia offended and alone, and that probably Lord Edward would be imposed on her as her partner for the night. Still, the ball was the ball, and with a final sob, and a throwing up her hands, as at the irony of fate, she turned away to surrender herself a willing victim into the hands of Nurse Ludlow, whose primitive ideas of dressing had resulted hitherto in the notion of a good wash, and who could now only stand by in wonder and admiration of her Missy's being so smart.

CHAPTER XII.

THE giving of a ball at E— Park was a great event in the calm times of which I write. Literally, months beforehand it was announced and commented on, the actual fixing of the day subject to deep astronomical and meteorological calculations as to the state of the weather, and the fulness of the moon.

When great county families drew out the family coach to drive twelve and even fourteen miles, it was quite necessary to ascertain as far as possible, if fords could be crossed, and that they would not be plunged in Egyptian darkness if the lamps went out; or in case of being attacked by highwaymen on Hartford flats, to see if possible clearly how many foes they had to point their pistols at.

Everyone visitable within possible distance expected to be asked, and were so in fact, for the popular duchess, prompted by the duke, was playing her cards to bring in her son, Lord Brownhill, for the county—and, though in herself the most exclusive of Tories, considered it good policy to begin by rallying all parties to the house. As to any little class distinctions which might prevail in country circles, she considered herself far too elevated to condescend to take cognisance of them—a largeness of view which did not pass without comment nevertheless among the small county dames which made up the neighbourhood. Drags full of officers were expected from Sandhurst in uniform, dear to the imaginations of ingenuous country misses, to whom the distinction of dancing with a pair of epaulettes qualified any amount of ugliness or dulness. Guardsmen from London were expected, and every unmarried curate and hunting clergyman within visiting distance; also every member of the Berkshire hunt, by special desire of the duchess, to appear in pink.

But among the neighbours it was the house-party which was the subject of the most eager solicitude,—to know who, or who not, among the famous beaux and belles who figured in the London news, were to be seen in flesh and blood. What they would wear, and how they would behave ? If any Royalties were to grace the ball, from Windsor or Bagshot, and, if so, what was the proper etiquette in case of need ? To be spoken to by a royal duke,—or a princess,—and be un-acquainted with the proper mode of reply, was a continency too awful to con-template. Whether Lord Brownhill would be present ?—he being a known hater of balls,—but such a good fellow,— his merry eyes had made many a rustic little heart beat,—and if so, whether he would wear his volunteer uniform, in which he looked so well, or appear simply in evening dress ? As to Lord Edward, he excited little curiosity. People spoke of him as a haughty lad with impertinent manners, quite wanting in the charm which made his mother and brother such universal favourites with all.

.   .   .   .

As Jane, after a long drive, seated oppo-site her mamma, in the recesses of the family coach, dashed under the lofty portico of E— Park, and entered the illuminated hall, through files of servants in gaudy liveries, a demure gentleman in black, the groom of the chambers, advancing to show the way,—she was filled with a trepidation that almost took away her breath.

'Now, child, don't be nervous,' whispered Lady Danvers, as they were being divested of their wraps by more elegantly attired gentlemen, also dressed in black. 'But, good heavens! where is your fan?'

'Here, mamma.'

'Now, mind and don't break it. And your bouquet, too,' placing in her hands some fragrant flowers. 'Knowing how you fidget, I have held them for you myself.'

'But, mamma,' whispered back Jane, quite overcome by the files of arriving ladies, rustling in opera cloaks and mantles, and the immovable phlegm of the attendants waiting to announce them, —'I do feel so awkward, I think I had better have my hands to myself.'

'Impossible; do as I tell you,'—arranging the flowers. 'I don't care for all these niceties myself, but the duchess does. Remember what I said about tumbling down. If you do anything

absurd, you will make yourself ridiculous
for life.   Get a nickname, or some
horrid thing which will make us both
laughed at.'

Nothing but the perfect composure of
Lady Danvers, looking the very type of
mature beauty, in a heavily falling robe
of red velvet, a white turban, on her well-
turned head, starred with brilliants and
pearls, reassured Jane.   Intuitively she
felt her mother was not one whit behind-
hand in the great world in which she
moved with the step and bearing of a
finished aristocrat, and this gave her
courage.

To her mother, therefore, she hung on
with a feeling of helpless dependence, as,
faithfully clasping fan, bouquet and handkerchief, she passed from a lofty ante-
room, decorated with banks of flowers
into the spacious ballroom, glittering
with innumerable waxlights, over a floor
prepared for dancing, so slippery every
step she took terrified her out of her
wits.   Well as she knew the house,—every
thing looked so unfamiliar in the unwonted magnificence, she stared like a
stranger, when the duchess, resplendent with jewels, and with a starred

coronet glistening like a firmament on her head, offered the tips of her delicate fingers, and in her gracious way saluted her with a kiss.

' How well our charming *débutante* looks,' was her greeting, eyeing Jane with a gratified scrutiny. ' Really, Lady Danvers, most successful,'—with a glance at the white tulle dress. ' I congratulate you. I hope, dear, you will enjoy yourself. I have placed you under the care of Edward.' Then, turning away to receive party after party of arriving guests, she left them.

After that the duke came forward to greet them—the blue ribbon of the Garter across his breast. A fair washed-out looking man, with a thin, aristocratic face, whom no amount of rank could make other than the ' husband of the duchess,' a matrimonial shadow, only gaining importance from that substance.

To Jane's infinite relief Lord Edward was not in sight, but Lord Brownhill came forward, leaning on a stick, still lame from his recent accident, to shake hands in his hearty way,—the most unaffected of the whole ducal party, and often discomposing his mother by his rough friendliness with what she styled '*individuals of the lower class*,' whose existence she would gladly, except at election times, utterly ignore.

'You see I am out of the running myself, Lady Danvers, but can I be useful in getting your daughter a partner?' he said, with a wry face at his wounded limb. Edward is loafing about, probably playing cards,' with a knowing glance at Jane, which made her blush scarlet. 'Shall I endeavour to find him and bring him up?'

'No, no, please not,' she cried, quite forgetful of what was due to her august mamma. 'I feel so shy, I would much rather sit down and look about me a little.'

Seen for the first time it was a study! The rich dresses of the ladies, specially of the dowagers', sitting round on velvet benches raised against the white and gold walls; the voluminous hats then in fashion, with masses of sweeping plumes, —the sparkling eyes, the heightened colour, the low, musical laughs, the brilliancy of the jewels, from the deep tint of rubies and emeralds to the softened sheen of pearls,—under the glitter of the enormous chandeliers; the unmoved dignity of the

wearers, looking like high-bred masks ;
the lovely artificial flowers on head and
dress, the waving of feathers to and fro,
the rustling of thick dresses as they swept
the parquet floor ; the red coats of the
hunt, and the decorations of diplomates
and peers,—formed as brilliant a tableau
as can be conceived. There were scarlet
uniforms of officers, hung with orders,
from Sandhurst, braided hussar jackets
hung over one shoulder ; guardsmen with
smooth, do-nothing-looking faces, super-
lative in gold lace ; the dark but graceful
uniform of the riflemen looking always
ready to mount and ride ; a bronze-faced,
stout-built admiral,—one of Lady Danvers'
reputed *pretendants*,—formed by nature
to pace the deck of a man-of-war ; an
ambassador, resplendent with jewelled
stars, talking and laughing in a loud
harsh voice ; Lord C—, the beau of
that day, rejoicing in a double row of
fair whiskers ; a tall judge, always draping
imaginary ermine ; a great lawyer, with
hurried step, as if on a continual circuit ;
the scarlet fez of a Turkish *attaché*, the
resplendent vest of a Magyar grandee,
famous for his ropes of pearls ; a cele-
brated poet and singer, whose last com-

position had excited the town into genuine admiration, short and vivacious, with a dark curly head ;—and many of the choicest of the *jeunesse dorée* of the day, who, protesting all the while about the bore of coming into the country, had still so far sacrificed themselves as to obey the duchess's invitation to join her distinguished party at the ball ;—and when the music struck up and the dancing began,—that *did* astonish the rustic mind of Jane, taught at an academy at R—, where she was deemed a proficient. Dancing indeed !—flying rather. This was another science altogether when, slippery as was the floor, pair after pair glided by in a sliding shadowy sort of movement, utterly dissimilar to the vigorous steps she had been used to, and she inwardly trembled, and her breath came short as she thought of trusting herself on this ice-like surface, among graceful forms that floated, light as a feather, in undulatory movements she longed, yet dared not attempt, to imitate.

All the men looked, Jane thought, prodigiously alike, except that some were old and others young. They had all the same affected smile, the same little laugh, the same mock attempt at being interested

about nothing, the same semblance of devotion meted out to all, the same phrases, the
same looks and gestures, as they changed
their partners and paraded up and down.

As she stood, a little behind her mother,
surrounded by her usual circle of elderly
admirers—looking on with intense curiosity,—a couple, fatigued by the dance,
passed near.

' How full the rooms are,' said the lady,
yawning behind her fan, ' and the heat
overpowering.'

' Quite so,' was the rejoinder ; ' but with
such a companion,'—with a soft glance
into the lady's eyes,—'anything is an
advantage which enables us to talk.
Everyone is at their best to-night. Of
course I include you,'—with another soft
glance, which the lady returned with interest. ' How do you think the duchess
is looking ? '

' Splendid ! That dress of green and
gold, and all those emeralds, are perfect.
She has two grown-up sons, yet it is
wonderful how she preserves her looks.'

' By-the-bye,' returned the gentleman,
' have you heard that there is an heiress
here to-night,—quite a raw little country
miss,—not yet presented ? I forget her

name, but Jack of the Blues knows her mother, and says she has a splendid old place down here, and at least ten thousand a year.   Quite the match of the season, I hear.'

'Have you seen her?' asked the lady, an involuntary coldness in her voice.

'No; and I cannot find anyone who has, though I know for certain she is here.   I have been looking out for a kind of "*Miss Hoyden*," without her dog, but, as yet, have seen nothing to match.'

'Ah! even if she is even ugly or awkward she is sure to find admirers,' said the lady, rather tartly.   'Poor little thing, she is certain to be sacrificed to a *mariage de convénance*, and be made miserable for life.'

'Well, I don't know,' was the answer. 'Jack says he hears she has a great deal of character, and is quite an original. Besides, report says she is already engaged to the duke's youngest son, Lord Edward.   Lord Brownhill, who is a capital fellow, looks higher, of course.   His brother has already, I hear, run into absurd debts at Eton.   He will spend her money by-and-by.   There are not so many couples dancing now,—will you have

another turn ?'—to which, the lady as-
senting, they dashed into the throng.

Listening to all this, Jane's heart beat
almost to bursting. No one had ever
told her she was an heiress, though, had
she been less simple, she might have
guessed it for herself. Ten thousand
a year,—that, she knew, was ridiculous;
but—well, it was all to be hers, though
her mother had never told her. For the
moment her heart leaped with childish
elation. Of course it was the money
and Faulds that made the duchess select
her. The dear duchess, to think she
could be so sly!—And Lord Edward, what
a miserable little cheat!

Scales seemed to fall from her eyes,
and it was with the greatest difficulty
she could contain herself. 'The match
of the season—engaged to Lord Edward!'
'Sacrificed to a *mariage de convénance !*'
—how it all ran dancing through her
brain!

Fortunately for her, her mother was
engaged in talking to Lord Brownhill, who was recounting his accident,—
and an unspoken animosity to her worldliness chilled her to the very soul.

'An heiress!' Just what poor Sophia

had been ; and now, everyone was making much of her and forgetting her cousin.

At that moment the name of Maitland caught her ear.

'Yes, by Jove!   But for Maitland it was all over with me.   The infernal brute had me under him,—a rare, fine fellow, full of pluck, and a splendid rider.'

'Maitland?' repeated Lady Danvers, looking up at Lord Brownhill swaying to and fro on his stick, as if he fancied he was on horseback.   'Does he live at Twickenham?'

'Yes, I think he does.   A rich old father,—rather vulgar people, I should say; but he is number one—A.   Do you know him?'

'Well, not exactly, but my sister does. I think I should like to be introduced to him, if he is here, specially,' she added, in her bland way, 'if he saved your life, Lord Brownhill.   That gives him at once a claim to my esteem.'

'Oh, that don't matter'—and he gave a hearty laugh—'to anyone but my mother. First-rate for Edward, you know, if I had been smashed.   But, putting aside all that, a capital fellow,—just the style I like.   I'll bring him up if he comes.   For some reason or other he has been quite surly the last few days. Some love-affair, I suppose. He is so good-looking. Didn't want to face the world, and all that rubbish. He said he would not come, but I made him promise. For my part,' added Lord Brownhill, with one of his hearty laughs, ' I don't think I shall every marry. I see men making such everlasting donkeys of themselves, when they are in love.'

' Marry without love, my lord,' said the curly-headed little poet coming up,—' much more rational.'

' What, such sentiments from you, Mr M—? I thought you lived on love.'

' Not at all. That is all shop. I don't believe in it. That is why I deal in it with such success. If I were hit myself, I should lose the trick.'

' Well,' said Lord Brownhill, ' if two such extremes meet as you and I, there must be something in it. From different premisses the same result. I wonder what your daughter thinks, Lady Danvers,' with a glance at Jane, who stood with round wondering eyes turned on the dancers.

' As yet I hope she has formed no opinions,' answered Lady Danvers gravely. ' That is to come.'

If the ball had appeared to Jane a scene of enchantment before, now she heard there was a chance of seeing Maitland, her paradise was complete — Maitland who, she kept repeating to herself, impressed and occupied her for Sophia's sake.   Maitland might ask her to dance, at which her heart beat wildly—and she could talk to him of Sophia, and her mother would ask him to Faulds, and Sophia and he would be reconciled—and then—

But no time was allowed her to work out the problem, or to ask herself what part remained for her when all was over. Her mother, in a circle of friends and neighbours, drew her towards her to take part in the conversation.   There was Lady Mac—, who lived in the large red house on the hill, opposite the terraces,— a sweet-faced lady in blue, a perfect Greuze, with a mass of fair ringlets, renowned in the hunt for her daring riding, —and Lady C—, with her cameo-cut face and deliberate manners.

'So glad to see you, Lady Danvers!' ran round.   'You shut yourself up so much.   Is this Jane?   How do you do? Your first ball?   Timid?   Ah, you will enjoy your next much more.'

Here a distinguished - looking man,
combed and scented like a barber, crossed
from the opposite side and astonished
Jane by bowing. Fully convinced he had
made a mistake, she did not return it.
Nothing daunted, he advanced and shook
hands with her mother.

'I fear your daughter does not recollect
me,' he said, contemplating Jane with a
stereotyped smile.

'Indeed, no—I beg your pardon—I do
not,' answered she, spite of her mother's
frowns.

'Perhaps,' he added, with a little amused
laugh, 'you would recall me better in a
red coat on horseback. However, permit me to stamp myself on your memory
in another dress by dancing the next
quadrille with you. Lady Danvers, do
you hear how I propose not to be forgotten?' and he gave another affected
laugh, to which Lady Danvers responded
by her most gracious smile.

'Who is that man so like a monkey?'
asked Jane, as he fell back among the
crowd.

'The Marquis of D—, you simpleton,—
the greatest match in Europe. You have
seen him over and over again at the hunt-

breakfasts. He is lively and agreeable
enough, if he likes, but abominably
airified.'

'You heard he has just asked me to
dance, mamma.'

'Lucky girl!' and Lady Danvers
smiled. 'This is a good beginning. You
will be the envy of the whole room.
Don't tear your dress, or slip, or otherwise
disgrace yourself. Here is the duke
coming up with Lord Edward;' and taking Jane by the arm she advanced to meet
them. 'Mind what you are about,' with a
glance Jane quite understood; but since
she had overheard that conversation, her
mother's glances did not affect her so
much. Was she not as worldly as all the
rest? Her childish deference and faith
were gone. Lady Danvers was her
mother, but henceforth she held her fate
in her own hands, and from that moment
she decided that no one should influence
her choice.

Far off the duke was seen approaching,
interrupted in his course by intervening
friends, and behind him following Lord
Edward, more ridiculously overdressed
and coxcomical than ever,—the most provoking air of superiority on his boyish face.

Jane glanced up at her mother—the diamonds on the white turban sparkling, the
tightly-gored velvet dress falling round her
in statuesque folds—with a fixed resolve
once for all to set herself free.

'If,' said the duke, bowing low as he
led his evidently reluctant son forward,
' our brilliant little *débutante* is not already
engaged many times deep, will she do my
son the favour to dance with him ? '

' Jane will be most happy,' answered
Lady Danvers, giving her daughter no
time to answer, ' if it is not the next quadrille.   For that she is engaged to the
Marquis of D—'

' Fortunately, it is a waltz,' said the
duke, putting up a diamond-set eyeglass
to look at the placard hung out before
the gallery where the band was placed.
' Edward,' to his son, with a pantomime of
offering his arm.

Perforce Lord Edward was obliged to
come forward, and the ill-matched pair
moved off.

' How well they look together!' whispered the duke to Lady Danvers, a gratified smile lighting up his faded face.   ' A
charming contrast!   Miss Danvers has so
much style and Edward such composure.

Her first dance and her first partner! That is just as it should be, only I hope it will be a partner for life. I suppose you and her grace will settle everything soon. For my part, I think the sooner the better.'

Lady Danvers bowed.

' I am altogether for an early marriage,' she replied, 'especially for a girl with money; one does not know to what temptations she will be exposed.'

' Quite so. I am sure Edward is most fortunate. We are all so fond of Jane.'

In a few moments the waltz began, and Jane found herself launched into the vortex of dancers. At first she forgot her indignation against Lord Edward and that she was 'the heiress talked of by the Blues,' and remembered only that she had never danced on waxed floors before, and was entirely ignorant as to how the figure was managed. Terrified and strange, she clung to the arm of Lord Edward, who, with a malicious pleasure in his steely-blue eyes, watched her embarrassment.

' You don't seem to like it much,' he said, with a laugh.

This remark gave her courage. After all it was exhilarating to make one among that brilliant circle,—to feel herself a unit among those hundreds of elegant women. The animation of the fine band, the glitter of the crowd, the intoxication of the atmosphere prevailed, and to her own astonishment Jane dashed into a waltz with a strange confidence, then, after a while, drew up to take breath.

'You are aware you very nearly slipped,' said Lord Edward, dropping her arm and taking out an embroidered pocket-handkerchief loaded with scent. 'You seem to be quite new to it.'

'And you?' answered Jane, resolved upon revenge, and feeling herself, as an heiress, full of courage. 'Does your father always choose your partners for you?'

Lord Edward winced, but made no answer.

'Has he so much power over you?' continued Jane, warming to the attack, as she noticed how crimson his face grew. 'How disagreeable it must be to be treated like a child! How glad you will be to grow older, and have a will of your own! For my part, though I am only a girl, I could not endure that sort of thing.'

Not knowing what to say, he writhed under her sarcasm, as she, with glowing cheeks, prepared to continue in the same strain. ('What does it matter?' she was saying to herself. 'We hate each other already as much as we can!') Then, eyeing him with a look of deliberate mischief, she continued,—

'I expected to see you take your brother's place to-night—as he is lame. I wonder how you would have done the honours? I suppose the duchess could not trust you. I never saw you at all when we came in. Are you shy? Or were you hiding?'

'I don't like dancing,' answered Lord Edward, becoming more and more sullen, under Jane's continued attack. 'I never do, if I can help it.'

'Then, why on earth did you ask me?' and she gave him a mocking glance which went far to move him into an uncivil rejoinder. 'I am sure I did not want it. I think we had enough of each other's company in the wood the other day, at Faulds?'

Lord Edward—from red grew pale— as he listened and remembered how his mother had lectured him all the way home, and a kind of terror of what she might say kept him silent. Not so Jane, launched triumphantly on the rising tide of her revenge : ' Why don't you learn to have a will of your own, Lord Edward ?' she continued, standing back from the circle of dancers—to make herself more impressive. ' Take my advice and assert yourself, as I mean to do—or something worse may happen to you than only *dancing* with those you don't like.'

A glow of angry colour, and a glitter in his eye, showed he understood her meaning. So enraged was he, that he dropped her arm, and would have left her in the middle of the room had he dared.

' I quite agree with you, Miss Danvers,' he said, trying to be composed, and succeeding but badly. ' No one shall dictate to me any more, I promise you. I have been a fool to permit it.'

' How glad I am,' laughed Jane, amused spite of herself. ' Only think of my being of any use to *you* ! You seemed to despise me so the other day. As far as I am concerned, Lord Edward, we are agreed. I intend to be free.' As the last notes of the waltz hurried to a close, she added, ' Our duty dance is over. Please take me back to mamma.' Then, with a significant glance, ' I think we understand each other ?'

' Perfectly,' was his answer, as he offered

her his arm, with a look as if he could have strangled her. 'Nothing ever was clearer. You will not find me *de trop* again.'

'Well, that is plucky for a school-boy— I beg your pardon—an Etonian. I don't understand the difference.'

What Lord Edward would have answered to this Parthian shot never can be known, except that an unmentionable word *did* escape him ; for at that moment the Marquis of D— came up and claimed Jane for his partner. The fates had combined to humiliate Lord Edward. The despised country 'Miss' to be carried off by the Marquis of D—! She left him with a look of triumph, and took her place at the top of the quadrille, conscious that every young woman in the room envied her. The marquis was most agreeable. He named and discussed all the London belles present for her benefit. Jane was in the highest spirits at the discomfiture of Lord Edward. Her simple notions amused her partner, and he laughed heartily at her *naïve* re- marks. She informed him it was her first ball. To which he replied that he per- ceived it was, with a bow and a smile, at which Jane blushed crimson, and making a false step, would have fallen, had he not held her up. To the quadrille succeeded a galop, which they danced together; and again Jane, in the wild delight of flying along the room, stumbled on the waxed floor, and again his arm saved her.

By the time the galop was over he had quite constituted himself her protector, and she felt genuinely grateful.

'Allow me to remind you,' he said, as he led her to her seat, 'that I have twice prevented you from falling. I only mention it in the hope that you will remember me with goodwill.'

'Oh! indeed I shall!' cried Jane, quite overcome at her awkwardness. 'For all that, I have thoroughly enjoyed my dance, because I was not frightened.'

'Really? Then, as we are near neighbours, I hope it will not be our last, Miss Danvers.'

And he bowed, and left her at her mother's side.

CHAPTER XIII.

WHEN Jane joined Lady Danvers, she found her in earnest conversation with a gentleman whose back was turned to her. Something in the graceful lines of the upright figure struck her as familiar, and when he looked round she found herself face to face with Maitland. Not beaming with health and exercise as she had seen him in the Red lane, but sobered and saddened,—his fresh colour faded, his cheek pallid and lined, and with a worn, haggard look in his eyes that quite changed their expression.

'My daughter, Mr Maitland,' said Lady Danvers, presenting Jane. 'I believe you have met before.'

Jane did not answer. She had involuntarily so carried his image in her heart, that when he appeared it seemed only in the natural order of things that he should be there.

'I was not aware,' he returned, bowing, a quick glance firing his dull eyes, 'that Miss Danvers had come out.'

'Nor has she,' answered her mother; 'but, at the request of the duchess, I made to-night an exception.'

At this moment Lord Brownhill came up.

'Ah! I see, Lady Danvers, you and Maitland are in *medias res*—a great deal to talk about, I daresay. Edward, old fellow,' laying his hand on Maitland's shoulder, 'have you disclosed to Lady Danvers the secret of your changed looks? You won't enlighten me. But I have some idea you will be more frank with *her*.' Then, in his rapid way, without waiting to mark Edward's evident preturbation, he turned to Lady Danvers, 'If you will put up with a lame cavalier, will you allow me to hand you to supper?'

As they moved off through files of couples preparing for a fresh dance, Maitland naturally offered his arm to Jane, who accepted it with such evident pleasure, he must have been blind indeed not to observe it.

The way to the supper-room led through

a splendid conservatory, illuminated by myriads of coloured lights concealed among thick, feathery fronds of palm, tree-fern, banana, and oleander,—a fairy scene that might have recalled the tropics. Umbrageous orange-branches drooped laden with golden fruit,—the citrons shone like pale lamps among the glistening foliage, —innumerable camelias formed into beauteous bouquets of white and red among the waxen leaves,—the yellow mimosa fell in fluffy ringlets, — lilies and geraniums formed perfumed banks, and the ground was covered with a mossy carpet, out of which every shade of hyacinth, tulip, and primula raised their crested heads. From a crystal basin in the centre a fountain rose out of delicious waterplants, in a perpetual gurgle,—to fall back in a foam of spray, glittering like silver ; and in a cunningly contrived rock-work, breaking the flowering shrubs, seats were set in darkest shadow among the clustering boughs.

Couple after couple passed down among the flowers,—rich robes swept upon the tessellated floor, diamonds glistened in the subdued light, the sound of low laughter and soft talk fell on the ear, and the distant notes of the band crashing through the entrain of a Viennese waltz gave life to the whole.

Even while hanging on Maitland's arm, Jane's eyes kept travelling round, insatiable in wonder and curiosity,—until stopping before one of the embosomed seats, Maitland, in a low voice, asked her whether she would like to rest a little before attempting to penetrate into the blazing supper-room beyond, where, on long and heavily laden tables, the magnificent plate of the house of Upshire was displayed under the flashing of countless chandeliers.

'Oh, so much !' she answered involuntarily, blushing. 'I am so glad to leave all these tiresome talkers, and have a quiet moment with you. I have so much to say about Sophia. Poor dear ! She is so ill.'

As her name passed Jane's lips, Edward's colour changed.

'Ill !' he exclaimed. 'What is the matter ? Surely nothing serious ?'

'I don't know that,' was Jane's diplomatic answer—her eyes fixed on him. 'That depends—I think she is ill because she is so unhappy.'

She stopped, and a very audible sigh came from Maitland.

'Are you not coming to see her?' she asked abruptly, puzzled at his silence and constraint, so unlike the ardour of young Delville—to whom she was involuntarily comparing him—when Cecilia was in such distress at the Blue Post Inn. Delville never forsook Cecilia.

A few moments passed before he replied, 'If I might presume to think my coming would be of service, of course I—'

'Oh, Mr Maitland, it would be life to her!'

'Lady Danvers has asked me,'—he spoke with evident reluctance, 'to ride over to Faulds to-morrow; if Miss Escott permits it, I will come. I hope I shall see you also,' he added.

A bright smile from Jane answered him. 'Oh, do come!' and she was about to assure him how glad Sophia would be—when, as if to avoid continuing the subject, he went on hastily to say that he was about to leave E—, but could not do so without paying his respects to Lady Danvers.

'And you,' he continued, turning to Jane —a sudden curiosity animating his look and gesture, 'I hear this is your first ball. Are you in ecstasies?'

Jane coloured and dropped her head in

a fixed contemplation of the now somewhat faded bouquet she held so religiously
in her hand.

'Oh yes, at first. It seemed like a
dream ; but I like sitting here quietly with
you much better than dancing.'

'Indeed !' answered Maitland. 'Then
you take a great deal of pains to appear
different from what you are if everything
lively does not please you.'

'Oh !' more and more confused, as she
found Maitland was contemplating her in
an earnest gaze ; 'that is for the moment.'
(A pause.) 'But if you knew me better
you would understand. I love to live in
my own thoughts—all sorts of ridiculous
fancies I make out alone. If you knew the
life I lead at home you would believe me.
Until Sophia came I used to bury myself
in the woods. Everyone laughs at me for
my day-dreams, and now I laugh at them
myself. Life seems so full of suffering—'

She stopped and raised her eyes.
Maitland's evident disinclination to speak
of her cousin blanked her. Fain would
she have retrieved her character as a
loyal friend, and deserve no more reproaches for want of zeal—absolute devotion to her cousin possessed her.

'Indeed! Is it possible?' returned he, with unfeigned surprise.

'Yes, indeed. All this gaiety is very amusing at first, but I could not live this kind of life, especially'—in a lower tone, venturing a glance at his resolute lip and finely-chiselled profile,—then looking down confused at meeting the full power of his serious gaze—'when I think of Sophia alone and miserable at home.'

An inexplicable look of pain pased like a shadow across his expressive face, and left it pale; but again he ignored Jane's allusion to her cousin, and continued,—

'Are you old enough to judge?' he asked. 'Young ladies of your age are not remarkable for consistency.'

He tried to call up a smile, but it was not a genuine one.

'Yes, that is true. But I want to people my world with very different beings to those I see here. I want some one to live for—to think of day and night— Since Sophia came' (at her name Maitland turned away and bit his lip until the dent of the teeth remained impressed on it) 'I have mixed her up in all my thoughts and actions. But much as I love her, she is not the companion I have dreamed of. That one once found, I should never change—no, never!' and her brown eyes looked out into immeasurable space.

'And,' asked Maitland, imperceptibly lowering his voice into a deep, harmonious tone that came thrilling to the ear of Jane through the varying measure of the distant music, 'have you ever fancied who this companion—this husband, I suppose, I must call him' (at the word husband Jane shook her head), 'is to be?'

She hesitated — she trembled — she thought it must have been fancy, but it seemed to her that he touched her arm as she sat under the gaudy walls of the pink oleanders, the glistening light, the gurgle of the lazy fountain giving a rhythm to her thoughts.

'Yes; I have seen one who, if he cared for me, would realise all my dreams.'

She stopped.—Where were her thoughts leading her? This was rank treachery, and the words rang in her ears like the confession of a crime. Maitland too grew strangely embarrassed, his face and manner became more and more reserved.

'Another time,' he answered, rising and leading her into the throng, 'you must

tell me who it is; you must allow me to
advise you.   However, if public report be
true, your choice is already made.   May
it be a happy one!'

It was not in the power of words to
paint Jane's chagrin.   Lord Edward, indeed!
Did he think she had given her heart to
him?   After all she had said he did not
understand her in the least; and of all
human beings she would best like to be
known by him!   Avoiding a gentleman
who was advancing to ask her to dance, she
drew Maitland into a corner, and whisper-
ing rather than speaking, lifted a pair of
glistening eyes to his saddened face,—

'It is most conceited of me to think
that you can care what becomes of me,
Mr Maitland.   I don't know why I have
been talking, but it is not as you think—
The one I mean'—again she stopped,
and positively shuddered at her own du-
plicity,—'is not the person you allude
to.   No—no; not at all.   I hate him!'
Her agitation made her voluble, and the
silent   attention   with   which   Maitland
listened.   'I have no right to mention
the other one at all; I have nothing to
do with him—I never can.   Please forget
what I have said.   It is folly.'

One by one, as she spoke, she was tearing out the freshest flowers from her bouquet. One by one—with her eyes vacantly fixed on the bright petals, and her head whirling with an unknown pain, as the rhythm of the distant music beat a wild measure in her brain.

'What lovely flowers!' said Edward, in a low voice, bending down to examine them until his sunny curls were on a level with her glowing cheeks.

'Are they not? The duchess sent them. I love flowers; they have a language to me of their own, specially outside in the fields. What things they say! They are the sweetest offerings to those we love. Even to the dead flowers are offered — how much more to the living!'

A dreamy confidence was stealing over her under the fascination of his glance. A rosebud and a heliotrope were in her fingers. Without daring to look at him, she placed them in his hand; then, seeing the duchess pass, she rushed off after her.

She heard his rapid step close behind, then she was caught up in the crowd, and except for a moment in the distance, she met him no more that night.

CHAPTER XIV.

NOT one word did Jane utter through the long drive home. She knew her mother was offended, and that feeling of exultation at her heiress-ship,—and the opinion of 'the Blues,' which had lifted her out of herself in the midst of that scene of enchantment—failed to sustain her now. For the first time in her life she had dared to disobey Lady Danvers, and she had actually laughed, and run away, when the duchess, with her sweetest smile, had made a special request that she should lead Sir Roger de Coverley with Lord Edward—and had taken refuge with Lord Brownhill, who, tired out with standing, was sitting in a corner. From him she learned that Maitland had left.

' Never saw a fellow so out of spirits,'
he added. ' Were you breaking his heart
afresh, Miss Danvers, when you were sitting in the rockery? You seemed to fit
very well.'

At which Jane crimsoned to her
temples.

' No ; certainly not.'

' Someone has been at work, then, in
good earnest. He is terribly cut up. I
wish I knew who it is. I would like to
give her a bit of my mind.'

So frank and friendly seemed Lord
Brownhill, Jane longed to tell him the
whole story. It was a very odd world
where the truth could not be spoken.
Honour and integrity were written on his
brow. He was Maitland's friend, and
would be sure to do good.

While she was debating in her own
mind what she should do, Lady Danvers
came up, and with that stern, hard look
she knew so well, seated herself beside
them, and whispered into her ear,—

' As you seem completely to have lost
your head, we had better go. Young
ladies do not leave their chaperones to
talk to young men, nor refuse the mistress
of the house what she desires. I am

ashamed of you.   Before supper I missed
you—now you have left me again.   Most
improper.'

' But, mamma ! ' ejaculated Jane,

' Don't speak in that loud voice, or
everyone will hear,' was the reply.   ' It is
quite enough that I know you have dis-
graced yourself, and greatly annoyed the
duchess.   Not another word.'

Then rising in her deliberate way, Lady
Danvers bid Lord Brownhill good-night
—amid many protestations on his part—
against the cruelty of taking Jane away so
soon.

' She must learn to submit to these
little sacrifices.   I am a bad chaperone,
and have a headache.   I don't see your
mother anywhere, so I will leave my
adieus with you.'

' So sorry, but won't you allow me to
find her ?   She will be quite hurt if you
don't take leave of her.'

' I prefer not,' answered Lady Danvers,
in that masterful way everyone was conscious of who came in contact with her.
' We have already given her too much
trouble—' with a significant look at Jane,
standing by, pale and silent.   ' Good-
night.   Do not rise.'

'By Jove! and I cannot hand you to your carriage! A thousand apologies? Where is that fellow Edward? In the card - room, I suppose,' with a sneer. 'That boy will turn into a court card some day, all over vermillion and paint. Let us hope it will be the King of Hearts, Miss Danvers, for your sake.'

But poor Jane, suddenly fallen from those empyrean heights of the heiress, talked of by the Blues, and become again an ordinary little mortal, turned on him such a pair of frightened eyes, he understood something was wrong, and said no more ; but with a friendly pressure of her small hand, let them depart through a side door, leading from the duke's study into the hall, the only room in that vast mansion that, at its master's earnest request, had been left undecorated and unlit.

. . . .

Lady Danvers sat a dark, immovable outline, framed in the carriage window just visible in the feeble moonlight. Rain had begun to fall, and there was a dismal moaning in the wind as they traversed the wide stretches of flat commons which lay between Upshire Park and Faulds, gloomy

with broad plantations of fir, so weird
and still, they looked like an army of
ghosts called out of the shadows of the
night, as the road rose and fell from
the open spaces into bosky dingles, cleft
by close lanes so dark and narrow that,
spite of the lighted lamps, nothing but the
slowest walking pace could ensure safety.
Not one word had passed between them,
and Nep's cold nose thrust into her
hand as Jane descended from the carriage seemed a joy. She stooped and
kissed his rough head.

'Ah, doggie, doggie, I fear our happy
days are past,' she whispered. 'No more
scampering for you and me. Trouble
has come to your little mistress, Nep,
—trouble she cannot help,' at which
the dog, licking her hand, gave a sympathetic whine. 'Yes; I believe you
understand me better than anyone else.
At least you love me, Nep. Good-
night.'

Next morning Jane was standing opposite her mother, installed in the dignity
of her own room, behind the barricade of
her large rosewood desk, which, from her
earliest days, her daughter had always

contemplated with awe as the depository of mysterious family secrets.

The stiff arrangement of the furniture was unpromising in itself. Everything placed to suit the central figure presiding as a judge. Nothing tasteful or cheerful. No scrap of colour. The heavy leather arm-chairs symmetrical; the barren tables strewed with papers and letters. The open grate with a smouldering fire, throwing out little heat. The large Elizabethan windows uncurtained, throwing a dull grey light against a clouded sky; a fresh damp breeze wafting in from the woods, joined to the strong perfume of a border of wallflower growing outside.

'Mamma,' said Jane, in a voice she vainly tried to render steady, her lips quivering nervously under the strain, 'I had better tell you at once. I am so sorry to vex you, but I cannot marry Lord Edward.'

'I expected this folly,' was the cold reply. 'Will you be good enough to impart to me your reasons, if you have any?' said her mother, turning on her a searching glance, much more terrifying than anger.

Jane had been prepared for reproaches,
threats, punishment perhaps, but this chilling contempt disarmed her.

'I—do—not—like—him,' she stam-
mered. 'I never can. As I am an
heiress—'

'Who told you that? Was it Sophia?'
came from Lady Danvers sharply.

'No, mamma, it was not.' (She was
gathering a kind of desperate courage to
proceed.) 'Sophia has nothing to do with
it. I found it out accidentally.'

'Accidentally! Some fool's gossip at
the ball probably,' drawing herself up
and spreading out her large white hands
with the glittering rings. 'You seem to
have acquired much experience there. I
suppose someone has caught your silly
fancy.' Jane coloured to the roots of
her hair and shook her head; her stiff,
frightened attitude suddenly changing into
soft lines of supplication as she leaned
forward against a chair.

'And does this accident, as you call it,
justify you in your own opinion in dis-
obeying me?'

'I think it does,' answered Jane meekly.
'I think the wrong would be to marry
anyone I dislike. Dear mamma, do not

quarrel with me. Some day or other I must
be a woman, and have a will of my own.'

'A will of your own!—A child—an
idiot!' cried Lady Danvers, bursting into
sudden wrath, provoked by the quiet
determination of Jane. 'What do you
know of life? What do you understand
by being an heiress? If I have not
hitherto told you that you are to inherit
your grandfather's fortune, it is because
I think money a misfortune to women,
and it has been my desire to educate you
with the utmost simplicity, to prevent
your head being turned. Now you know
all. Of course at my death Faulds will
be yours, but the bulk of your fortune
comes from your grandfather, who died
before you were born.'

Jane listened with downcast head.
Something seemed to shock her in hav-
ing forced all this from her mother.
Lady Danvers continued,—

'Does this knowledge exonerate you
from your duty to me?'

'No, no, mamma.'

'Well, and what is to be the practical
result? Do you suppose I shall repeat
this nonsense to the duchess? Are the
careful schemes I have laid for years

to be overturned by the freak of an inexperienced girl? Because you are independent do you intend to defy me? You will understand your marriage is to take place in a year.'

Lady Danvers, no longer able to maintain the mask of indifference she had assumed, rose and paced slowly up and down the room, pausing from time to time to watch the effect of her words.

'Remember I am your guardian, at least for the present. I can deprive you of the means on which you count. Have a care, child, not to provoke me too much. Tell me the truth. You like someone else. Who is it?'

'No, no, mamma,' cried Jane, throwing herself before her, her loose, brown curls falling like a veil over her face; but, taking her firmly by the hand, Lady Danvers placed her on one side, as though removing a useless impediment from her path; 'no one, no one. I only want to use my liberty not to marry Lord Edward. Don't press me. Don't hurt me,' she cried, bursting into tears. 'I don't deserve it; I have difficulties enough.' And the scared, bewildered look on her young face would have appealed to anyone less severe than Lady Danvers.

'After all,' she continued, not heeding Jane at all, 'I have only myself to blame. I might have known the result of bringing Sophia here. Her insolent pride was sure to teach you rebellion.'

Full of remorse at the effect of what she had said, Jane was about to rush forward to exculpate her cousin, when again Lady Danvers imperiously put her back.

'You are too ignorant to understand the mischief you have caused. I cannot reason with a fool,—I can only command her. Do you think, after this proof of the effect of her presence here, I will allow Sophia to remain? I have told her that she must either marry or go away. If she ruins her own prospects I cannot help it. It is my duty to protect yours.'

'Oh, mamma, mamma,' cried Jane, casting herself at her mother's feet, her piteous voice rising above Lady Danvers's loud tones. 'It is not so. Punish me—kill me, but do not blame Sophia.'

'Don't be ridiculous. Her fate is in her own hand; there are many courses open to her. If she will not marry, she can return to my sister, or go out as a governess.'

'A governess! Oh, mamma, surely you would not allow that. Why am I to be cared for and petted and she despised? Mamma, mamma, have mercy. Have mercy,' pleaded Jane. 'It was I who brought her here.'

'What! more rebellion,' cried Lady Danvers, reddening with anger; 'every word you say only convinces me of her influence! You never dared to speak to me like this before. If you turn against Sophia—'

'I never will,' cried Jane, whose warm heart beat indignantly at her mother's injustice. 'I must have my own money some time. She shall live with me. I have promised never to forsake her, and I will keep my word.'

'Child, your folly is really incomprehensible. You have read novels until you transform all life into a romance.' Mr Maitland is coming to-day. Why should not Sophia accept him? It is a very simple way out of all difficulty.'

Then, as if a sudden thought struck her, she advanced towards the lofty hearth, carved and painted to the raftered ceiling, the armorial shield of the Danvers conspicuous in front, and rung the bell. The sound echoed through the silent house like an alarum.

'Tell Miss Escott,' to the servant who came hurrying in, 'that I request her to come down and speak to me at once.'

'Have mercy,' pleaded Jane, turning an agonised little face towards her mother; 'let *me* tell her. Do not provoke her.'

Ere Lady Danvers could reply or meet the wildness of the childish grasp which was laid upon her arm, a sound of clumsy footsteps in the passage outside came nearer and nearer. A door banged overhead violently in a distant room, several voices were heard outside, and the wrinkled face of Nurse Ludlow appeared at the door.

'She's gone, my lady!'

'Gone!' echoed Jane, turning ashy white.

'And nothing she left but this bit of trumpery paper in her room, — "Tell Lady Danvers I am going to Scatlands." Robert spelt her out before you sent for her just now, and I looked in, and the bed never slept in, and she sitting so quiet when I took her her tea, when you and Missey were at the ball. The sheets folded as I put 'um, and her long cloak off the peg. Oh, Missey' (in reply to an agonised look from Jane), 'don't look at me as though you'd eat me! 'Tis no one's fault, my lady,' curtseying to Lady Danvers. 'I cannot help it. She were a high 'un—God Almighty knows!'

'How dreadful!' cried Jane, rousing herself from the lethargy of fright into which she had fallen, and devouring the paper with her eyes. 'Let me go after her, mamma. I will take the next coach to Twickenham. I shall get there almost as soon as she.'

To read Lady Danvers's face was at all times difficult, but now, sitting with that paper in her hand, it was so inscrutable, that Jane stood, as it were, suspended, her very soul in her eyes.

'This is no matter for a child to meddle with,' she said at last. 'Without a great deal of care, this may be magnified into a great scandal. In my position, I cannot allow my name to be mixed up in such an affair. Sophia has released me from all responsibility—the consequences are on her own head. What is proper shall be done. All I ask of you is to leave me alone. Did no one see her this morning?' to Nurse Ludlow, who stood smoothing her

white apron with shaking hands, watching
Jane, whose bloodless face was the image
of despair.

'No, my lady; nought saw her go,
only the lodge-keeper's son, who is in
the hall, do say, when he brought the
milk, that a young lady in a long cloak
passed through the park gates with her
veil down, and took the high road about
the same hour as the " Lightning " coach
passes to London. Mabbee the young
lady had some 'un to meet her. She were
allers sly.'

Here a furious glance from Jane silenced
her. Many, as has been said, were the
battles Jane had fought with the old
woman, who hated what she called
Sophia's ' Hindjan ways.'

'That is enough,' said Lady Danvers,
in a voice of authority, pointing to the
door; 'I want nothing more.'

'Gone, all alone!' cried Jane, wringing
her hands, an overwhelming feeling of
remorse coming over her as to how far
she herself might have contributed to
drive Sophia to this rash act,—then, as
she stood, weary-eyed and stricken, before
her mother, occupied in addressing some
hasty lines to be sent express to her

sister,—'Mamma, I don't believe you are a bit sorry Sophia is gone. It is a shame —a horrid shame!'

Lady Danvers looked up.

'Be silent, Jane, or I shall send you from the room.'

'I don't care where I go, or what becomes of me,' was her answer; 'I brought her here, and she has been driven out the very day that Maitland was coming. Poor dear! she did not know. People call me an heiress—a pretty heiress! If I had but a shilling of my own I would go after her and bring her back!'

'Not here!' cried Lady Danvers, roused to attention by Jane's repeated attacks. 'Not into my house, much as I regret the manner of her going; no inducement shall prevail on me ever to receive her again. I shall send a servant with a letter to Amelia to assure myself that she has arrived safely. Do calm yourself, you foolish child,' to Jane, who had covered her face with her hands to hide the hot tears which streamed down her cheeks; 'she will be taken good care of; and I will acquaint Mr Maitland with what has happened. Very awkward

for me, all the same,' she added. 'I hope
no one will know it, especially the
duchess, who would ask me no end of
awkward questions.'

Jane, her moist eyes now raised to her
mother's, listened, but in her own mind
decided that she alone would break the
news to Maitland. She would watch in
the park and catch him before he reached
the house.

'No one but me! no one but me!' she
kept repeating, and with this phrase beating on her brain, she sprang up, flew
into the hall, and down the terrace steps
to find relief in the open air. The sky,
the clouds, the fresh blasts of air re-
vived her. The fir-trees stretched their
huge branches to comfort her ; the scent
of the woods calmed her. But oh, grief
and sorrow, how hard it was to bear !
Oh, tender blossom of returning love,
blossoming as on the verge of a volcano,
to be dashed and deadened by the despair
of the one poor heart for whom its petals
had opened !

No bonnet on her head,—her dress
saturated with dew,—Jane wandered on,
listening to every sound. The wood-
pecker tapping on the trunk, the squirrel's

shrill squeak, the cooing of the wood-pigeons in the depths of the wood, the low, sad note of the sandrake far out on the heath, the rooks cawing to each other as they circled round the trees,—sound, sight, sense, all rising out of that nameless flush of colour and greenery which hails the spring!

A little shower fell, then the sun struggled out, but she waited on hour after hour, her heart cold within her lest Maitland should not come, her eyes fixed on the approach—her ears dull with listening for sounds which would not come.

CHAPTER XV.

MEANWHILE Edward Maitland was riding slowly down the long lime avenue which breaks from the main road through the lodge gates at Faulds, the road rising and falling in umbrageous lines as the architectural boughs close in a thick network overhead. As a man lost in thought, he sat low on the saddle, the chequered light casting shadows on his anxious face, so fixed and resolute, with that look of power in the massive moulding of the brow, and the firm lines about the mouth and chin—a man this not to yield to what he thought wrong, or be swayed from side to side by any force of argument brought to bear upon him. Yet, calm as he seemed, he dreaded, though he longed, for this interview with Sophia. In the grief of not seeing her, he had forgotten all the bitterness of the struggle he had passed through; the harsh words which he had meant to say died on his lips. He had decided to tell her that the old love was killed by her pride. But, behold, it was alive! Ready to burst into flame at her command. Should he at once ask to see Sophia, or plead his cause first with Lady Danvers? In these days of waiting he had resolved to appeal direct to his father; that excellent, though homely man, would, he knew, see right done. A violent breach with his mother would be the result, and accusations and reproaches that would break up his home. But that was not all. A terrible fear haunted him that it was all of no avail; that, do what he would, Sophia would never change.

Why, he asked himself, had he so persistently repelled the gentle endeavours of her little cousin to make peace? He had thought about her a good deal, and the desire to ask her why she had left him so abruptly at the ball seemed to take an undue preponderance in his mind. Those flowers she had placed in his hand—he had them still, pressed into a letter which

he had carried ever since, and a feeling of
pain came over him when he thought of
her young life sacrificed to a marriage with
such a scapegrace as Lord Edward.

With his head sunk on his breast he
rode on, his horse's steps making no sound
on the moist gravel ; his course now and
then arrested by the beauty of some special
vista in the breaks of the glorious old chase,
or as he emerged from the wilder portion
of the park, to dismount in order to un-
fasten some gate, beyond which sheets of
emerald lawns spread out.

Suddenly he was arrested by a slight
rustle, and the figure of Jane rose before
him, her lips open trying to speak, but
failing in the effort.

' She is gone,' she cried at last, holding
up her hands. ' Sophia—she went before
she knew—'

Here her voice broke, and clasping her
fingers together she sank upon the ground.

' She loves you, indeed, she does. She
did not know you were to come.'

To Maitland the truth flashed in a
gleam like lightning ; but the blow was so
sudden, the thing so bewildering, he could
only stare at Jane, and repeat Sophia's
name.

' I brought her here. I did it. I would have sacrificed anything for her and you : and now, without a word, she is gone ! I love you better—I mean *her*, it is all the same — than all the world.'

She stopped, half choked. Maitland looking on, his face working in indescribable emotion.

' Where is she ?' he asked at last, Jane cowering before him, her face in her hands. ' But no one can blame you, Miss Danvers,' he added, gently raising her from the matted grass. ' Only try to tell me where she is.'

' At Scatlands,' was the reply. ' I wanted to go, but mamma would not let me. She has sent a messenger. Sophia left a line to say she had gone there.'

Then she gathered her scattered senses together, and told him how it was, his own eyes melting as in an unsteady voice she continued,—

' Oh yes, I am alone to blame. I vexed her, and I wronged you.'

' Wronged me, Miss Danvers !'

' Don't interrupt me,' she cried impatiently, bracing herself up to a great effort. ' I want to tell you—I want you to know the worst. It is not her fault at all; I came here to say so.'

He looked at her in the utmost amazement. Even in the heaviness of his heart, at this crowning act of Sophia's passion, the interest he felt in this strange girl was for the moment uppermost.

Jane, in spite of the encouragement she was giving herself in her heroic scheme of self-sacrifice, felt her heart sink lower and lower. How could she form the words? Would he see it in the light she wished—as against herself? It was part of her purpose to paint herself blacker than she believed herself to be to exonerate Sophia.

'We quarrelled,' she said, in a hushed voice, catching at her breath as Maitland came nearer, his eyes riveted on her face. (He was her friend now; in another moment he would hate her. That winning face, so tenderly indulgent as he waited for her words, would change to reproach and anger; but it must be done.) 'Yes, we quarrelled, because she was jealous, and thought I cared for you. Oh, Mr Maitland!'—in a tone of sharp anguish—'will you ever forgive me? It was her love for you that made her go.

You will believe me? You will follow her, will you not? And oh, do remember to tell her that it was I, her little Jane, who made you understand it.' (The dearest thing she had on earth, she knew it now —it came to her in this speech—was slipping from her. She seemed to clutch it while she spoke.) 'And you will never forgive me'—stretching out her hand— 'You cannot!' ('He will curse me,' was in her thought, 'now I have told him what a wretch I am.') But she waited in vain for any change in his countenance. Amazement was there — bewilderment, pity—as he caught at her hands to steady her trembling form—nothing more.

'And you did this?' he said slowly. 'But surely you are in jest?'

'Oh no, no!' she exclaimed, in a voice of anguish. 'Do you think I could jest about such things? I thought you understood it at the ball, when I ran away. You—you should never have known it from me, but that Sophia is gone. But you will go to Scatlands?'—drawing herself away—for the first time her cold cheeks crimsoning with blushes. 'You will see her— Promise me to go and comfort her.'

'Can you doubt it?' was Edward's

reply, eyeing the confused little figure
before him with a glance so mingled of
pity and interest it was hard to say
which feeling had the mastery. ' I will
follow her at once ; but you'—and as he
spoke he turned the full power of his deep
grey eyes upon her,—'you are alone.
Good heavens ! your clothes are dripping ;
your feet are wet.' For the first time he
noticed her uncovered head, her dishevelled
hair, and the wildness of her aspect. ' How
long have you waited ? '

'Oh, hours,' she answered in a low
voice ; ' but that does not matter. I am
used to waiting in the wet. I was so
afraid that you might have your mind
poisoned by mamma.'

'Yes ; Lady Danvers,' said Edward,
with an abstracted air. ' Ought I not to
see her ? '

'Oh no, no !' shrieked Jane, roused to
a sudden horror lest this ordeal which she
had so carefully prepared should be thrown
away if they met, ' Not mamma ; I will
make some excuse. Do not see mamma.
Sophia wants you ; go to her.'

'But, Miss Danvers'—Edward was
unwilling to leave her without a word,
yet not knowing what that word should

be, lingered,—'at least let me thank you for your confidence before I go. I feel quite unworthy of it.'

It was his turn to blush now, and his comely face darkened with the rush of blood that swept through him like a wave.

'Believe me that your generous conduct'—here he stopped, his ideas so confused he scarce could mould them into words—'shall never be forgotten. I am ashamed of the cause as being my most unworthy self, but I appreciate the motive.'

'Oh, never mind me,' cried Jane, calling up the ghost of a smile. 'Besides, what is it but to make amends for the wrong I have done? It is so good of you to forgive me, but I cannot forget that it was I who really divided you. It was most wicked; but I did—at the ball. Sophia found it out. She questioned me.'

Then her heart swelled within her as she looked into his face, and felt she was for ever cutting the ground from under her own feet.

'No, you did not divide us at all,' he replied, gazing with infinite pain at the working of her features, some conviction of the truth coming to him from her strange inconsistency. 'No, Sophia herself raised a barrier, no one else.'

He would have wished to say more, but something within him forbade it.

'Still,' urged Jane, 'but for me she would be here. Lose no time, Mr Maitland,' pointing to his horse ; 'never mind me,' in answer to an inquiring look round, as if in search of some one with whom to leave her, 'I am used to be alone.'

'But I *do* mind,' he replied, speaking with unwonted warmth. 'Whatever has happened—and I confess I cannot yet altogether understand what it all means—you will permit me to assure you that you will ever be to me a subject of the deepest, the dearest interest. Not Sophia Escott herself can shut out the memory of this day.' Then in a calmer tone. 'We may meet again, when all this trouble will be forgotten ; but remember, Miss Danvers' (and his thoughts struck off in the direction of Lord Edward, and his firm impression that she was engaged to him), 'you will ever find a brother in me. Call on me whenever you like ; I will answer. Good-bye.'

Taking her hand, he raised it to his lips, and remounted, turning to cast a last glance at the palpitating little figure, backed by the shafted branches of the

trees.   Like a ray of tropical sunshine,
that approving look shot through to her
innermost being.

'No, no,' she murmured, as his tall
figure gradually dwindled and disappeared
into the shadows of the avenue.   'He
does not despise me.   I do not repent
what I have done!'   And something of
the old joyfulness came into her face the
first time that day as her eyes wandered
round instinctively in search of something
that was missing.   'Why, where is the
dog?' she cried. 'I must have been lost,
indeed, not to remember Nep;' but
if his mistress had forgotten him, Nep
had not forgotten his mistress.

As if sympathetic to her thought, a wet,
touzled head, with blood-shot eyes, appeared at that moment, pushing through
the matted ranks of fern and briars,
barking wildly as he caught sight of her.
Then bounding forward, he precipitated
his whole weight upon her.

To say that he was a happy dog was
not to express half.   He was a dog de-
lirious with joy.   Where he had been, and
in what spot he had sought her, was his
secret.   His long hair was stuck through
with brambles; his body saturated with wet.

One leg so bound up by a thorn he limped when he thought about it, but not else.

'Down, Nep, down,' cried Jane, staggering under his weight, as, with tongue extended and outstretched paws, he peered into her face, giving, as she shook him off a little roughly, one of those plaintive little whines with which he was wont to relieve his feelings under the sense of wrong.

This was too much for Jane. Clinging to him as if he were her only friend, she pulled him down to where she had seated herself among the leaves, and, burying her face in his rough coat, burst into such a fit of tears that if ever dog was initiated into a knowledge of human woe, surely that one was Nep!

CHAPTER XVI.

IT was a sultry evening for the time of year.

The wind swept fitfully across the Twickenham meadows, and dark clouds were rapidly impelled forwards by high currents of air. Up from the river came low mutterings from the osier and willow beds, and the big elms in the hedgerows, swaying in the evening light, cast deep shadows on the thorns, green with the first leaves of spring.

A dark, tall figure appeared for a moment on the high road, then turned quickly down the lane, not taking the open in the middle, but shrinking along those ragged little tracts of grass under the damp walls.

Either illness or weakness made her steps uncertain. Every now and then

she stopped and gazed round, then seeing
no one, moved on again, with a languid
motion, her arms hanging at her side,
her head cast down.

Who would have recognised the haughty
Sophia in this crushed and dejected figure,
as step by step she advanced like some
wandering spirit revisiting the scenes from
which its mortal essence had disappeared?
Gate after gate was passed of the many
cheerful villas bordering the lane, their
bright display of flowers lighting up the
gloom of the laurel and yew hedges that
screened the road.

At last the gaunt form of the house of
Scatlands rose to view, with its flat Anne
windows staring like unlidded eyes, the
monotonous lines of white mortar on the
deep-toned bricks traversing the front,
the head of the Roman Emperor, in its
niche, dominating the range of upper
windows, and that pervading look of
penury revealed in the scaling paint of
the woodwork, and panes of cracked glass
in the windows here and there.

Arrived at the green door breaking the
garden wall, before which she had watched
for whole days, conjuring up a form that
never came, Sophia paused, her aching

brow hid in her hand. She did not heed
the big drops of rain that had begun to
fall, nor the tearing of the wind, lashed by
the gusts coming up from the river, which
played with her dark hair, bringing out its
glossy richness. How long a time passed
she did not know ; it seemed to her suddenly to have grown very dark, as she
raised her hand to the bell, then shrank
back. The first time she had stood there
on her arrival in England, Maitland was
by her side. Should they ever meet
again ?

At last the bell sounded. What had
she done ? What would they say to
her ? And with what words should she
reply ?

And then she knew no more until she
found herself in the yellow drawing-room,
opposite the picture of San Sebastian,
with those holy eyes bent on her, and
Aunt Amelia's arm round her neck, as she
tenderly placed her on a chair. ' My love,
my love,' murmured the poor little woman,
with ill-suppressed tears, the ribbons on
her cap trembling with emotion. ' How
ill you look !—what has happened ? '

' Ask me nothing to-night,' was Sophia's
answer, spoken so low Mrs Winter leant

her head down to catch the words. ' I have come away.'

' Does my sister know it ? ' asked Aunt Amelia, not able to overcome a feeling of alarm at the idea of receiving Sophia against Lady Danvers's will.

' By this time she does,' was the answer, as she lay back half fainting, her face white and bloodless, with broad black shades under her eyes. Then, with a touch of the old pride, she raised her head. ' I have done nothing wrong, Aunt Amelia. Do not be afraid ; I have only come away.

' Wrong, my poor child ! No ! no ! ' and Mrs Winter's warm heart gushed up, and flushed her pale cheeks, under the tresses of the delicate fair hair.

(Aunt Amelia looked thinner and more careworn than before. Louis Winter had again got into trouble, quarrelled with his partner Gompertz, and attempted to raise money upon the works of art confided to him, a fraud which fortunately John Bauer stopped. Then he made a great *coup* by discovering that a picture hid away in a warehouse was an undoubted Titian, and the dealers came in again and reinstated him in the old way at Scatlands.)

' I am sure,' repeated Mrs Winter emphatically, ' my regal Sophia is incapable of wrong.'

A deep sigh was the answer. Then Mrs Winter rushed out to fetch wine, tripping herself up in her haste across the hall, and altogether losing all knowledge of her keys, quite snug in a corner of her pocket all the time, a fact she at last discovered. Jacob had been turned away, after much altercation on his part, occasioned by the irregular payment of his wages ; there was no one in the house but a maid-of-all-work, far away at that moment in the depths of the kitchen.

To behold her magnificent niece so fallen filled Mrs Winter's benevolent heart with infinite compassion. She was aware that her sister and Sophia did not get on, but this unexpected return was utterly unaccountable. Something terrible must have happened. How she longed to ask !

Then Sophia sat up a little and looked round. Yes, it was all very peaceful. There was the tall window, where the robins came to be fed. Moses and Pharaoh amid the plagues of Egypt in the blue Dutch tiles of the grate ; beautiful pictures beaming from the walls ; the large china jars filling the air with a subtle aroma of rose leaves ; the little mandarin figures, with pig-tails ; the scuffled Dresden ladies, in reds and purple, in impossible attitudes ; the yellow curtains, partly drawn to shade the light ; the well-worn shagreen case, with Uncle Louis's silver-mounted flute, lying on the piano ; the torn piles of music—just as if she had not been absent a day.

Aunt Amelia was so bewildered, and her heart beat so, she could hardly speak, when Sophia, in a low voice, asked if Uncle Louis was at home.   (The old fancy had come over her that he represented her father.   Oh, how soft to be cradled like a suffering infant in his arms !)

' No, my love,' answered Aunt Amelia ; ' he is dining with John Bauer.   What will he say when he hears you are here ? Could you not have let us know ? '

' John Bauer,' repeated Sophia absently ; ' he is a good man.   Does he ever speak of me ? '

' Speak of you ?—why, surely he does ! John will never alter ; he worships the very ground you stand on.'

But Sophia did not hear.   She was absorbed in her own dark thoughts.   The aspect of the room, and the sound of Mrs Winter's voice, brought back the past so vividly, she seemed to be standing again in the doorway, watching Maitland in the hall, with that wild desire to fling her arms round him and never let him go!

'Aunt Amelia,' she said at length, speaking very low, 'you must forgive my silence. I think I have been ill. All day in the coach my head felt like lead. I am very glad to come back,' a faint smile playing round her lips. 'But,' in an almost inaudible voice, 'it will not be for long.'

'Bless you for saying that, my child. How you reward me! You must never go away,' and in that one instant the generous heart forgave all the wrongs Sophia had made her suffer.

She only saw in her her dear brother's child. She would have given all she possessed to ask what it all meant, and why Sophia had left Faulds; but her delicacy forbade it. Something there was so strange about her; her beautiful features were so set, her face so bloodless and waxen, her movements as of one so unconscious of what she did, Aunt Amelia contemplated her with a kind of awe. Never could she hope to approach to familiarity

with her brother's child, superb even in
her sorrow. And she heaved a sigh,
drawn from her heart of hearts, at the
abyss which lay between them. And
thus they sat for a while in silence, the
old ebony clock ticking in the hall quite
audibly between the gusts of wind roaring
round the corner of the house and the
clatter of the rain dashing against the
panes.

'Tell Uncle Louis,' said Sophia, rousing
herself, 'that I am tired and cannot sit up.
I should have liked to have given him a
kiss. Tell him that I leave him my love.
My love,' her eyes wandering towards the
door, 'and my thanks; and to you, too,
my aunt.'

'But, Sophia,' cried Mrs Winter, 'you
have but just come, and you talk as if you
were going away. Surely, *now*, you will
never leave us.' Anxiously she laid her
hand on Sophia's shoulder and looked into
her face. Something she saw there which
silenced her. 'My dear, are you suffering?'
she asked hurriedly. 'What is it?'

'Nothing,' was the answer; 'I only want
rest. Shall I find my old room?'

Then from the lethargy in which she had
sat, a sudden impatience seemed to seize

her. She started up and hurried towards the door.

' Yes, certainly, my love,' answered Mrs Winter, following her. ' It has never been touched since you left. I told my sister that if you were not happy you should always have a home here.'

Now they had passed the hall and were on the oak stairs, Aunt Amelia going first, carrying a candle ; Sophia treading rapidly in the shaft of light, the bare stairs creaking under her footsteps and waking strange echoes in the empty house. A door on the first floor stood open, and showed a frame of darkness against the light, and as they mounted higher and higher, the wind sounded louder and louder among the passages under the roof. So quickly did Sophia press on her aunt that the poor little woman paused, panting, at the top, and drew back to let her pass, her tall figure forming itself into a shadow so dark and spectral it engulfed the space. Then she stepped proudly into her room and closed the door, forgetting altogether poor Aunt Amelia, who, terrified, without knowing why, lingered outside, trembling on the landing, her heart throbbing wildly against her side.

How she wished Uncle Louis was at home! How late he was! Never had the old familiar stairs frightened her before, but now a spirit of evil seemed abroad that turned her cold. At each door she passed she expected to see it open to disclose some unearthly form. Every weird and horrible tale she had ever read came suddenly to her mind and seemed about to be enacted before her eyes. Ashamed of herself, she came down, followed all the time, as it seemed, by ghostly footsteps. The hall, too, looked strangely black, and the wood-work in the oak panelling cracked as the light she carried cast fitful gleams into the corners. Nor did she recover herself until arrived at last in the comfort of the yellow drawing-room, where, ensconced in the depths of her bee-hive chair, she laughed heartily at her own folly.

CHAPTER XVII.

WHILST Aunt Amelia slept in peace, after having with difficulty prevented Louis Winter, who came home late, a little elated by all the good things John Bauer had pressed on him, from rushing bodily into Sophia's room—('Amalie, zee ees von beasts,' he kept repeating, as he tore off his clothes, 'to shut me out von die blessed schilds! Is dees not my house —not yours?'—until fatigue and sleep overcame him, and loud snores cut his speech),—Sophia stood in the darkness by the open window, looking towards Rosebank, in her old place, heedless of the torrents which drove in upon her and wetted her to the skin, or of the wild wind which seized upon her hair, casting about the long black tresses like serpents round her head.

Such a stormy night!—the stars hidden by drifting clouds, no moon, a spectral light through rifted breaks, the tempest howling away amongst the trees at Rosebank, swaying them to and fro ; the river swollen into tiny waves, lapping the bank ; a tall poplar close by, darkening the space, its trembling leaves, like souls in pain, shivering in the blast. Leaning against the sill tumultuous and awful thoughts passed through her brain, but all vanished before the crushing reality of her abandonment.

'Oh, my God, I cannot bear it!' she cried, flinging herself down. 'Let me die!'

Her heart leaped up, then stood still. For a moment her pulses ceased to beat. She seemed hanging in space, seeing nothing, feeling nothing, only that sense of terrible sorrow over her, as the end grew near.

'Edward, Edward!' she murmured, then laughed bitterly. Was this his truth and honour? 'No more my Edward, what do I care for else?'

She gave a cry, and leant her forehead

against the cold wall.   A sudden sensation seized her of sickening dread, as she
raised her hands to her bosom.   Yes, it
was there safe—her salvation.   Nothing
had changed but herself.   There were the
open lawns she had gazed on so often,
the blanched outlines of the house he
lived in rising up a white mass,—a wide-
spreading oak dark against the sky, a
flickering light from some boat upon the
river, and a distant hum of voices as of
revellers' return.   Her whole life rose
before her.   What a ruin it had been!
As the last look of a drowning mariner,
all was plain.   In a flash of unreal light
she saw it all.   Life might have been very
sweet,—she was so young.   It might have
come laden with joy.   Her soul seemed
to yearn for happiness, floating on the
nameless sea of the unknown.   Was the
end then so near?   The vision faded out.
She was dreaming with her eyes open.
Again darkness closed round her in walls
of eternal night.   To sleep for ever!—No
more weary time, but eternity in peace!—
No more hopeless longings.—No more
visions of happy times—all done!
    Again she turned to the window, leaning
against the sill, her face white and rigid,

with widely-opened eyes looking out into the night, with an attention so fixed the impression of the smallest object burnt itself into her brain.

No sooner was she in her old place again, than a sudden distress came over her. A black cloud swept down and engulfed her. There was neither sun nor moon in the dark world in which she stood. She groped in darkness, as in a rayless vault, knowing not how she came there or how she was to go. Oppressed with horror she raised her eyes, and what she saw turned her to stone. Out in the wild night was the outline of a dark turbaned head. She could not see the face nor shape of form or arm. A pair of dusky hands spread out and almost touched her. The apparition stood for a moment, then passed, and Sophia knew that Zebula was there. The time was come. She had appeared to call her. Her eyes filmed over and her head swam. She had just strength enough to clutch the filigree bottle so long hid in her bosom, raise it to her lips, and pour the poison into her mouth.

.   .   .   .

While Aunt Amelia slept and dreamed happy dreams of a more cheerful home, and John Bauer as a bridegroom in new clothes, leading her out to dance in the dragon-room, while Uncle Louis played the flute and the ice-figure of a woman looked on—Sophia lay face upwards to the sky.

Low mutterings sounded from the west, and a mysterious rustling in the leaves as of human voices among the trees. What wild spirits of the night ran shrieking through those woods; or was it but the echo of the thunder in the blast? The black lips of the clouds shot out lightnings, and gusty rain drifts raged through the open room, tearing up carpets and draperies, and flinging them over her where she lay.

Let the storm come thicker and faster and wash away her pain! Let the lightnings burn it out as they played around! And as the wind rose, and great thunder-claps smote the land, and the rain poured down on her as she lay, her cold hands clasped upon her eyes, sweeter far was this tempest and tumult than the mocking peace of her life; for, if the Angels of Death were abroad, who to her was so sweet as they?

.   .   .   .

Aunt Amelia's poor little robins flocked for shelter among the leaves, and the cattle in the meadows huddled together for shelter under the trees, and still the thunder roared louder and louder, and the lightning flashed fiercer and fiercer, in the wild turmoil of the night. Then the grey-eyed dawn stole forth and there was a great calm. The winds lulled, the lightnings stayed, and the thunder growled forth its last note ; the rain drops from the Anne windows fell wearily drop by drop, and the clustering woods lay silent, every leaf lulled to rest.

Even so was she beautiful in death, as she had been in life, with only a little dark stain upon her lips just touching the marble pureness of her cheek. No look of pain or fear on her young face, which, even breathless and inanimate, kept its thrall, but the calm majesty of peace in those widely-opened eyes never more to smile, and on the chiseled features on which the anguish of pain and weariness had sat so long.

CHAPTER XVIII.

'AND have you heard,' said the duchess to her friend the blue-eyed Lady Mac (who out of her saddle was the greatest gossip going), speaking from the twilight of her boudoir at Upshire Park, as she leant back on a settee of pink brocaded satin, the same material with which the room was lined—shedding a delicate reflex upon her pale aristocratic features, a little more worn than when we last saw her with the battles of fashionable life, but still winning and gracious as heretofore,—'have you heard of the strange marriage Miss Danvers is about to make ? Quite out of her set, I understand. Some low man.'

'Heard of it,' cried the lively Lady Mac, who always sat in a lounging manly way as

if the remembrance of the saddle haunted
her, ' I should think I have. No one has
talked of anything else at the meets. The
Staff College is full of it—even the cadets
—I declare I am quite sick of it. At the
horse sale on Tuesday, where I went to
look at some colts, no business was done,
everyone forming into knots to discuss
the engagement of the Berkshire heiress.
The young men are furious she has not
chosen a stranger.'

' I did what I could for the girl,' said
the duchess, just a little curl of contempt
forming upon her well-cut lips ; ' a strange,
wild little creature whom no one would
ever have looked at but for her fortune.
I could make nothing of her ; her tastes
are decidedly vulgar.'

' No wonder,' rejoined Lady Mac;
' Lady Danvers let her run quite wild.
" A hardy out-door education," she told me,
when I met Jane miles away from home one
day out hunting, sitting under a hedge
with a very disagreeable dog, who did his
best to throw me by dashing at my horse's
legs. The idea of a young lady with
ten thousand a year, and such a lovely
place as Faulds, being brought up like a
squaw !'

'Exactly,' said her grace; 'I could be of no use,' crossing her hands and playing with her finger-tips. 'Brownhill's position as member entails sacrifices, but I detest people who live out of my sphere.'

'But I thought,' said Lady Mac, who, though adoring the duchess as the great lady of Berkshire, had what the French call *un grain de malice* in her composition, which she could not always control—'that Jane Danvers was intended for Lord Edward. People said they were engaged at the ball you gave two years ago, —or was it three? Really, duchess,' with a gay laugh, adjusting some lovely flowers at her waist, 'you give us so many splendid entertainments one forgets.'

'Nothing of the kind,' answered her grace taking up one by one some priceless Dresden cups on the richly-inlaid buhl table, which screened her off, as it were, from a too close contact with visitors of less blue blood—and examining them as minutely as if she had never seen them before. 'Not at all the person I should select for Edward.'

'What! not an heiress?' insisted Lady Mac, not in the best taste, but her ladyship was not always in the position she occupied now. Rather obscure, in fact, in point of pedigree.   Some said the daughter of a circus master, but that was all nonsense. Still, a little wanting in refinement.—'I thought heiresses were born for younger sons.'

The duchess bridled like a majestic swan, which swells its snowy bosom to the flowing tide, then calmly composes its plumage, and sails proudly on.

'Ah! you mean a kind of barter,' a distant intonation in her voice. 'I hate that kind of thing.   I know it was said; but my son never dreamed of Miss Escott —he is too fastidious; nor would the duke have liked the connection.   Anything eccentric disgusts his Grace.'

Lady Mac longed to continue, but dared not. This was a little strong in the duchess when every one knew that the marriage was arranged at her own desire, and only postponed till Jane was older.   And every one also knew that Jane had so violently protested against being married against her will, that it was rumoured she had come over alone to Upshire Park, and had told the duchess that she would run away if it were insisted on—a threat it was known she was quite capable of putting into execution.

'And who is the person?' asked the duchess, after a pause, during which the two ladies sat opposite each other, somewhat like two polite athletes studying where the next home-thrust should be made. 'I hear he is not a gentleman. Do you know him?'

'Well,'—with a peal of that silvery laughter, which so often sounded from afar, after she had taken some desperate leap, and was congratulated on her pluck,— 'I certainly do meet many odd people out hunting, and in the stables, but the person in question is also known to you, duchess. It is the same Mr Maitland who saved Lord Brownhill's life. I have met him here in this house, at the same ball of which I spoke just now.'

For once in her life the duchess, woman of the world as she was, was nonplused, and generously owned her defeat before the statagery of Lady Mac, by a movement of the most unfeigned surprise.

'What! is it *that* Mr Maitland? I was not aware. But,' casting herself back on the pile of many-hued Oriental cushions gathered at her back, 'he is quite a nobody,—some city people's son. Of course I am obliged to him, but that does not

alter his birth—and not so very rich, I hear.
Well,' in a moment of annoyance she
could not repress, ' if Lady Danvers con-
sents to this she must be a fool.   Mr
Maitland,   indeed!—Lady   Danvers   is
really throwing her daughter away'

'Lady   Danvers   cannot   help   it,'   said
Lord Brownhill, entering from the library
beyond,   his   heavy   figure   and   broad
shoulders   sharply   defined   against   the
rich   binding   of   the   books,   arranged
in   elaborately   carved   bookcases   (the
library at Upshire Park was a superb gallery   of   the   time   of   James   the   First);
and shaking hands with Lady Mac, whose
bold   riding   and   pleasant   ways,   to   say
nothing   of   her   blonde   beauty   and   soft
violet   eyes,   made   her   a   great   favourite
with the members of the hunt.

'And   let   me   tell   you,   dear   mother,   you
must never forget, if you care for such an
unworthy   duffer   as   myself'   (the duchess
winced,—she   always   did   at   Lord   Brownhill's slang), 'what that man did for me.
He   is   my   bosom-friend.   One   of   the
noblest   fellows   God   ever   made.   You
must remember my speaking of him—'
(the   duchess   murmured   that   Maitland
was such a common name).   'Well, don't

forget it now,' said Lord Brownhill gravely, entering and stretching out his long limbs as he seated himself on a delicate spindle chair which gave an ominous crack at the weight imposed on it. ' He has been shut up ever since,—a perfect recluse,—saw no one but his father and me. I would not be excluded, and so at least he got used to me. A most romantic story, a beautiful girl nobody ever heard of, a niece of Lady Danvers,— she had her staying at Faulds,—who came from India. She must have been a mad kind of creature. Was engaged to him, and took some offence at his not marrying her straight off on account of his mother, who wanted a great match.' (Lady Danvers gave a little laugh, in which Lady Mac joined. Lady Mac always did join in ridiculing people who wanted great matches in order not to remind the world of her own.) 'And, by God! she went off and poisoned herself. He was quite off his head for a time, called himself a murderer, and all that. The fact is, it was not his fault at all, except being over desirous to do his duty. He was deuced fond of her, but the vio- lence and fury of the girl herself, who had Indian blood in her, her mother being some Rajah's daughter Mr Escott married out in India. Well, Jane Danvers, it appears, was very much attached to this cousin, and she took on, too, in the most tremendous manner at her death. She had taken a fancy to Maitland also when he came to Faulds, and between one and other, she was at death's door.

'Why, Lady Danvers told me nothing of all this,' exclaimed the duchess. 'To be sure I don't see her often now, and she has been away.'

'Jane Danvers is a little brick,' continued Lord Brownhill; 'she hid it all she could. Seemed like treachery to her dead cousin. But at last old Danvers pinned her,—I should not like the process myself,' and he laughed and again stretched out his long legs, producing another ominous crack from the over-weighted chair. 'And she confessed; then Maitland was sent for, and there was fainting and hysterics,—and God knows what a shindy you women can kick up—Lady Danvers declaring all the time in her most majestic way that she never would consent (for his people are rather low). Maitland was furious and went away; but the little girl got so ill Lady Danvers took her off to some warm place for the winter. But the cold was in her heart, poor little beggar, not outside! And so her mother found at last, and that she must make up her mind to lose her, or to consent to her marrying Maitland. He came to me about it, to ask my advice, dressed in the deep mourning he had worn ever since the cousin's death. He followed her coffin as chief mourner. He insisted on it, poor fellow, and fainted at the grave. But you are not attending to me, mother,' to the duchess, who had raised a sparkling hand to her mouth to suppress a yawn.

'Oh, do go on!' cried Lady Mac, her violet eyes turning in that seductive way towards Lord Brownhill she knew produced such an effect.—' I am so interested, specially now that *you* come into the story.'

'Very flattered, I am sure,' said he, 'but it is a case of love me, love my dog. I want you to care for my friend.'

'Oh! I do immensely,' said Lady Mac, a soft ogle in her eye. 'I want so much to hear what you said to him—something judicious, I am sure. Since you have become a member I look up to you so much.'

'Well,' continued Lord Brownhill, not

much pleased at the turn the conversation was taking—Lady Mac was clearly making capital of it for her own benefit,—' to make a long story short, " My dear fellow," I said, "you can't mourn for ever. The lady you loved has been dead two years. You have led a devil of a life since. Do you care for the girl ? " For a long time I could get no answer out of him, but at last a letter came to say she was much worse and wanted to see him. " Do you care for the girl ? " I asked again. At last he said he did, in a brotherly kind of way (never could love any other woman, and all that), and that she had been very kind and generous to her cousin, who, as far as I can make out, Lady Danvers treated very ill. " Then, for the sake of all that's blue, marry her," said I. " If you are such an Adonis that all the women run mad in love, don't kill off a second." You know, Lady Mac, I like my joke, but Maitland got very wroth, and said I had no feeling. Well, that is neither here nor there. He *has*, and he went off to visit little Jane Danvers, as good a little creature as I ever knew—to say nothing of her fortune, which Maitland wanted her to leave away, or some trash or other, to show he did not want it. And now they are to be married, and I am to be best man.'

'My dear Brownhill,' cried his mother, with vexation, raising herself up from the embroidered cushions, on which, with an air of infinite *ennui*, she had been resting, 'when will you leave off mixing yourself up with common people? Really, at election times it is bad enough, but to go on always!'

'Well, mother, you surprise me. Would you have me cut the man who saved my life because his father is not a peer? Maitland is a perfect gentleman. I wish some of our nearest and dearest were as good as he.' (This evident thrust at his mother's favourite, Lord Edward, who had at that moment contracted gambling debts to the extent of fifty thousand pounds, which the duke had to pay— silenced the noble lady.) 'And now, my dear mother,' rising and taking her hand, which he reverently kissed, then stroked with his long bony fingers, 'I know I am a great brute, with my rough ways and canvassings and elections, and that in your goodness to me you waive your feelings,— but I am going to ask you no end of a favour.'

The duchess's eyes rested on her elder-born with a certain pride. Spite of the constant annoyance he caused her, his large-hearted, generous nature impressed her with the charm it did everybody else. As he stood there, not aristocratic indeed in one sense of the word, but the image of the strong, burly Englishman, whose pluck and courage conquers the world, she looked up and smiled at him.

'Don't tax me too heavily, Brownhill,' she said, with an almost girlish grace, which made her even now attractive, 'and I will try.'

'I want you to be present at the marriage,' he said. 'Considering your former intimacy with Lady Danvers, and the brush you had with Jane, refusing Ned' ('all the better for her,' in an undertone), 'I think it would be but gracious.'

Was ever such an inconvenient son?

The Duchess was suddenly seized with a difficulty as to what to do with her eyes, and dropped her head to hide the blush which rose to her cheek.

'Well, what do you say?' he demanded eagerly, all unconscious of the mistake he had made, and which delighted Lady Mac so much she was inwardly deciding to whom she would first tell it as an excellent joke.

'No,' said the Duchess, rising to break up a conversation which, to her, had become a downright defeat. 'No, I think not; at any rate, we will speak of it another time. Come, Lady Mac, don't go. I know Brownhill will come with us if you stay. I want to show you my camelias; they are lovely just now. I don't think you have seen the new house the duke has put up joining the conservatory. I quite live there, I declare.'

'Yes, you must give me a lapful of those flowers,' said Lord Brownhill, following Lady Mac, who, as she rose, had managed to give him a good view of the most bewitching little ankles in the daintiest of stockings. It was not the first time certainly he had seen them, but still a good thing is always pleasant to look at; and so Lord Brownhill thought as they had a little interchange of *badinage*, and he managed to press her hand.

'Do you hear, mother? Plenty of camelias for the wedding next week.'

'Really, Brownhill, you are too fatiguing with your friends. You positively pester me. I will give you the flowers, but on one condition—that you do not once mention Jane Danvers again.'

. . . .

But the Duchess's good heart prevailed, at least under her son's direction. She *did* go to the wedding, and was most winning, Lady Danvers receiving her advances very coldly. She was a person never to forget a social affront, and the Duchess had dropped her ; but her Grace presented Jane with a magnificent bracelet, and kissed her, and a few months after received her and Maitland on a visit at Upshire Park, and gave a grand dinner (at which all the ducal plate was displayed), and a tremendous speech was made by Lord Brownhill to drink their health, to which Maitland responded for himself and Jane.

THE END.

COLSTON AND SON, PRINTERS, EDINBURGH.

www.ingramcontent.com/pod-product-compliance
Lightning Source LLC
Chambersburg PA
CBHW030800020726
47499CB00006B/1702